5/19/11
$15.95
I

8/11

MEXICO CITY NOIR

MEXICO CITY NOIR

EDITED BY PACO IGNACIO TAIBO II

translated by Achy Obejas

AKASHIC BOOKS
NEW YORK

This collection is comprised of works of fiction. All names, characters, places, and incidents are the product of the authors' imaginations. Any resemblance to real events or persons, living or dead, is entirely coincidental.

Published by Akashic Books
©2010 Akashic Books

Series concept by Tim McLoughlin and Johnny Temple
Mexico City map by Sohrab Habibion
Assistants to Achy Obejas (translator): Sarah Frank and Elise Johnson

ISBN-13: 978-1-933354-90-3
Library of Congress Control Number: 2009922935

First printing

Akashic Books
PO Box 1456
New York, NY 10009
info@akashicbooks.com
www.akashicbooks.com

Also in the Akashic Noir Series:

Forthcoming:

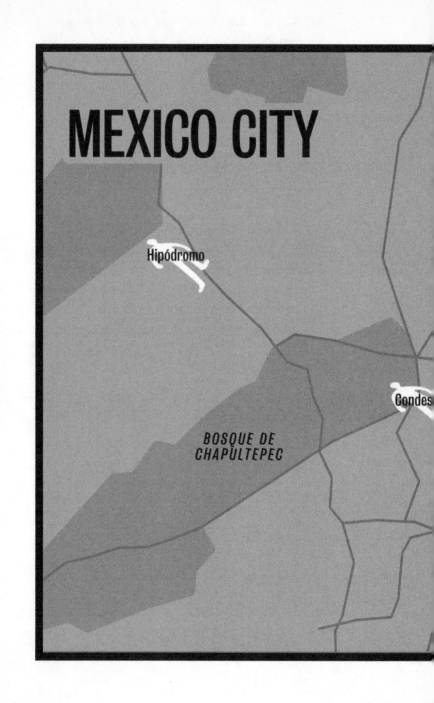

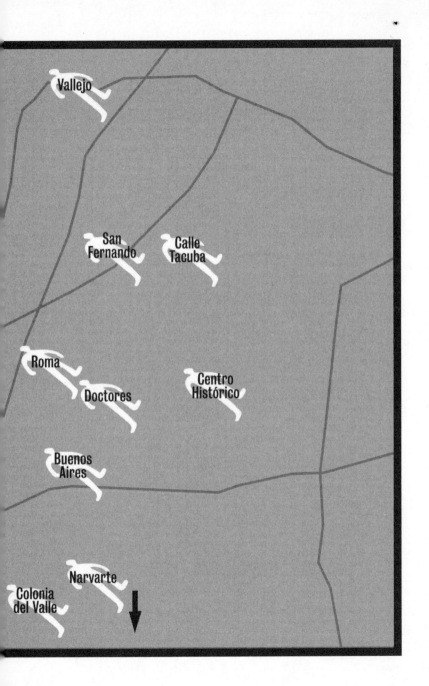

TABLE OF CONTENTS

PART III: SUFFOCATION CITY

INTRODUCTION

SNOW WHITE VS. DR. FRANKENSTEIN

I

Twenty-one million residents in the metropolitan area. An infinite city, one of the biggest in the world, a fascinating blanket of lights for those arriving on planes; a huge Christmas tree on its side—red, green, yellow, white; mercury, tungsten, sodium, neon. A city gone crazy with pollution, rain, traffic; an economic crisis that's been going on for twenty-five years.

A city famously notable for the strangest reasons: for being the urban counterpoint to the Chiapas jungle; for having the most diverse collection of jokes about death; for setting the record for most political protests in one year; for having two invisible volcanoes and the most corrupt police force on the planet.

Mexico is talked about more in jest than in earnest—how local law enforcement agents made martyrs of torturers in Argentina, how they bribed corrupt Thai cops, how they taught Colombian narcotraffickers to snort coke. But the rumors are miles behind reality. Here, a timid Snow White dictates the police report to Dr. Frankenstein.

To put memory in order, let us recall: in the early 1980s, the city's chief of police, General Arturo Durazo Moreno, was in charge of chasing down a gang of killers associated with South American drug dealers who were found massacred in a blackwater collector in the city's sewage system. The case provoked waves of newspaper ink, and the police suggested that it could have been a settling of scores between Central American gangs. A couple of years later the scandal resurfaced, and this time General Durazo was indicted. He was accused, among other things, of having given the order to kill rival Colombian dealers. The assassin, in that magical alchemy that is Mexican insanity, turned out to be his own prosecutor. His second-in-command, the chief of the state police, Francisco Sahagún Baca, was the head of the antidrug force, though he himself was one of the most notorious drug traffickers in the country.

The paradox: heaven's door in Lucifer's hands. Evil is everywhere. Each year, hundreds of police officers are fired, attempts are made to democratize Mexico City . . . but the cancer keeps metastasizing. Authority within the city depends on the police, no matter how corrupt they are. Now, in the name of modernity, everyone's uncomfortable with this. They don't know what to do. When the Division for the Investigation and Prevention of Delinquency was disbanded some twenty years ago, a spate of robberies inundated the Valley of Mexico. There were sixty-one assaults with a deadly weapon in a six-month period. The ex-cops turned a section of the city into their own turf. But it was just a small transition. As a matter of course, when they were still active officers, they had extorted, abused, robbed, and raped. Every now and then they went after some thief who operated outside of their jurisdiction. As ex-cops, they continued doing the same thing, perhaps pushing the envelope a little bit.

If you're lucky, you can stay away from it, you can keep your distance . . . until, suddenly, without a clear explanation of how, you fall into the web and become trapped.

What are the unwritten rules? How can you avoid them? Survey question: how many citizens do you know who, when assaulted on the street, will call the police? A few, none; maybe one of those boys in blue who patrols the intersections of this newly democratic city? A secret cop? Not on your life. What do you want, to be assaulted twice?

How big is the Mexico City police force? They say fifty-two squads. How many are officially sanctioned? How many bodyguards, paramilitary forces, armed groups associated with this or that official unit are there?

You wake up in the morning with the uneasy feeling that the law of probabilities is working against you.

II

You're going to die, the guy tells the man on his knees, and he repeats the phrase, showing off the gun barrel. The kneeling man, who's bleeding a bit from the bridge of his nose, doesn't respond; he reflects that, yes, he's going to die.

Hours later, when he tells his story to a pack of sleepy journalists, he thinks that, yes, he died, he died a little.

The man is Deputy Leonel Durán, member of the Party of the Democratic Revolution's (PRD) National Council. Some-time in July 2007, a black car cut off his vehicle at an intersection. Using both a pistol and an automatic weapon, they made him get out; political threats got tangled up with the vulgar assault, they threw him in the trunk, beat him, stole his credit cards, drove all over Mexico City with him imprisoned back there; they took his watch.

In the end, they left him in an open field, after threatening to charge him with running away from the law.

One of his cards was overdrawn and was therefore swallowed by the bank machine. This infuriated the cops most of all.

III

Toward the end of the '90s, a series of rapes that followed a certain pattern took place in the southern part of the city: a group of armed men would assault a young couple. First the robbery, then the rape. They usually stuffed the boyfriend in the trunk of a car. All the rapes were followed by death threats. Terror was practiced without reason—apparently, just to see what it felt like to wield the power of death itself. In a few cases, things got out of hand: a girl was strangled to death, an aggressive boyfriend was shot, another one asphyxiated in the trunk.

The majority of the rapes weren't reported. That was traditional. But in one case, the victim was the daughter of an important political operative. There was a police investigation. Other young victims emerged and recognized their assailants in a police photo album.

In a photo album of known delinquents? No. It contained pictures of political operatives. The gang of rapists consisted mostly of members of Assistant Prosecutor Javier Coello Trejo's bodyguard corps; he was deputy to the attorney general of the republic in charge of antidrug operations. The guys had too much free time sitting in parked cars, hanging out by building entrances, lounging at the homes of politicians. They had to pass the hours somehow . . .

Several of the killer rapists went to trial, others remained free. The assistant prosecutor was let go from his post and transferred to the Office of the Federal Prosecutor for the Consumer. There he could go after those who upped the price too much on video cassettes.

IV

Can it be that the black cloud of pollution that runs in the fast lane from the northeast to the southwest slowly drives us crazy?

Yet there's something beyond madness here: discipline. In Santa Clara—the industrial zone in the city's far north, a neighborhood full of chemical slush and loose dirt—a patrol car waits at dawn for the workers to emerge from the grave-yard shift at the Del Valle juice factory. The laborers have once again each received a small allotment of canned juice from the company. It's a miserable concession to union de-mands in a time of crisis. The cops stop them a few meters from the exit and steal half of what's in each worker's box. They stuff the cans in the backseat of the patrol car until it's full and they leave, the engine in low gear.

One day I saw the workers get together to protest their treatment by throwing rocks at the police. The cops didn't retaliate, they just left. Do they sell the juice to a little store in some nearby neighborhood? Do they take it home to their families?

V

In these last few years, the winds of change have blown through Mexico—citizens have more power, protests have managed to kick out the old administration. But they have only been able to improve relations with the cop on the corner, not defeat the march of crime.

The madness comes back with new variations. Now we have a killer of old women, a cannibal who eats his girlfriends.

VI

A cop stops me. My motorcycle is missing a mirror. I'm not willing to pay a bribe. We both laugh at how forthright I am. He tells me he has to pay for that corner. His supervisor charges him a weekly sum. If he doesn't pay, they send him to a worse corner, without traffic. Plus, he has to pay for whatever goes wrong with his motorcycle, and he has to do it at a private garage—in the police shop they steal the new parts and replace them with used ones. He also says that he goes out every day with only half a tank of gas, though he has to sign a receipt that says he received a full one. I tell him I'm not going to pay a bribe. He refuses to give me his name. I refuse to give him mine. We wait, it starts to rain. He gets tired of me. With a wave, he tells me to go. He smiles. There's not even ill will, it's all routine.

VII

Paloma, my wife, comes home in a fury and tells me a story about two guys she overheard reading headlines from a magazine in front of a newsstand.

The conversation goes like this:

Man #1: *He stabbed his wife forty-two times. Forty-two times, bro.*

Man #2: *Can you imagine? She must have been driving him nuts . . .*

My wife is indignant. She adds that, to top it off, the men didn't even buy the magazine.

VIII

A couple of undercover cops come to your door to tell you they've found your car but wonder why you haven't reported the theft. In fact, you didn't even know your car was missing. You peer out the window to check if it's true, that your car has vanished from where you parked it the night before. They tell you again that they've found the car. And where is it? you inquire. They give you the runaround. They finally ask for 10 percent of the car's value (marvelously, there are fixed rates)—that is, if you want the car back; if not, they'll drive it out of the city . . . and that's that. If you have insurance you tell them to go ahead; but if not, you're caught in the trap. Your car is worth 90,000 pesos and you've got to put 9,000 on the table. You're now certain that these two characters sitting in your living room and drinking your coffee have stolen your car, checked the papers, and are here to do a little business. You assume that this type of transaction is a daily occurrence for them.

IX

There was once a marijuana trade here. Domestic product. Mexican names for unregistered brands: Acapulco Gold, Tijuana Black, Oaxaca Small. I sense that it's gone now and that more alcoholic traditions have taken over. The narcotic seemed to disappear when hippies became bureaucrats during the economic crisis, and it's only occasionally at a rock concert that you smell weed in the air. Heroin never got much of a foothold in Mexican society. Every once in a while you hear about a case, but it's rare, and people talk about it as if it were something out of Hollywood, an extraterrestrial that no one entirely believes in. Cocaine, the yuppie and executive drug, provokes gossip and nothing more. The rumors sometimes become isolated newspaper articles. Here and there they say the white stuff floats around in Televisa bathrooms. There's a story about a movie star who needed surgery to reconstruct her nasal passages, and another one about the comedian who hosts children's programs and has to snort a little before facing the cameras to tell his jokes. But hard drugs aren't a part of everyday life—although they're available in just about all of the middle-class nightclubs. Here, the word "drug" is more associated with trafficking than usage.

We're the great airplane hangar, the way station to the United States for tons of marijuana, kilos of cocaine. Local and South American product crosses the border on ghost trucks, right past blind customs officials.

Narcotraffickers in Mexico City find themselves persecuted and uncomfortable, but powerful. They show off their gold bracelets and sip cognac in the company of cops. The trained dogs at Mexico City's airports usually can't get past the smell of Loewe cologne.

On other corners of the city, human throwaways roam the streets for everyone to see, stuttering kids only five, eight years old, with glassy eyes, hands and faces smudged with dirt. There are thousands of them. They're called "chemos"—they inhale chemical solvents like paint thinner and turpentine, they get high from sniffing glue in plastic bags. It's the drug of the lowlife, of misery. For a few pesos they sleep forever. The neurons die. Life is shortened.

X

Violence isn't usually part of humanity's social fabric. The economic crisis pushes more of the neighborhood waste to the city's center. On Zaragoza Street, in the eastern part of town, assaults on buses by kids with knives became quite common in the '90s. They robbed workers coming home from their jobs, maids, folks who worked in the markets. Hordes of desperate adolescents would descend on Santa Fe, one of the city's poorest areas, and steal from beverage trucks. But the neighborhood has changed: today it headquarters the new bourgeoisie. In the grocery stores around Lomas de Chapultepec, right in the heart of Mexico City's millionaire's row, a different style of robbery emerged over the last decade. Men would steal from women returning home from shopping; they would confront them in the underground parking lots, armed with the tools of their trade—screwdrivers, picks, scissors—and they'd ask the women for the bags of food. But they rarely took the car, or money. It was theft caused by hunger. In the last few years, there have been fewer of these; social programs have been slowly having an effect.

XI

I've said many times that statistics reveal a surprising city: one that has more movie theaters than Paris, more abortions than London, more universities than New York. Where nighttime has become sparse, desolate, the kingdom of only a few. Where violence rules, corners us, silences us into a kind of autism. Shuts us in our bedrooms with the TV on, creates that terrible circle of solitude where no one can depend on anyone but themselves.

XII

The writers in this volume aren't afraid of trying to exorcise the demons. Though using very different narrative styles, what they have in common is that they speak to, and about, a city they love. They understand that the only way to stop the violence and abuse that surrounds us is to talk about it. They are all professional writers but they are also professional survivors of life in Mexico City. Almost all of them, of us, take refuge in humor, a very dark humor, acidic, which allows us enough distance to laugh at Lucifer.

Another shared element in the stories that follow is an interest in experimentation, in crossing narrative planes, points of view. The neodetective story born in Mexico is not only a social literature but also one with an appetite for moving outside the traditional boundaries of genre.

Mexico City Noir may not be sponsored by the city's department of tourism, but if anyone, from anywhere on earth, were to ask whether the writers recommend visiting Mexico City, the response would be both firm and passionate: "Yes, of course."

Because this is the best city on the planet, in spite of itself.

Paco Ignacio Taibo II
Mexico City
October 2009

PART I

ABOVE THE LAW

I'M NOBODY

BY EDUARDO ANTONIO PARRA
Narvarte

Feet moving: a step, another, then one more. Eyes stare at the squares that make up the sidewalk. Stubborn hands grip the supermarket cart carrying all his things: a poncho, a plate and a pewter spoon, two shabby blankets, a plastic cup, a sun-bleached photo of a woman and a boy, a sweater, a paper bag filled with butts and three cigarettes, barely worn sneakers, a bottle with traces of liquor, several pieces of cardboard, and two empty boxes. His life: what remains of it. He pushes. He moves forward, barely registering the faces passing in the opposite direction. I don't look. I never pay attention. I haven't seen a thing, chief, I swear. Around here, I don't even look at the houses or buildings, just the street signs to know where I'm going. He walks on, not listening to the roar of the engines, or the screams of the horns around the public square, or the voices, or the screeching of tires. I'm nobody. No. I didn't hear anything. I never hear anything. He was a skinny thing, you know. He doesn't notice the food vendors, even though they arouse something in him, at the bottom of his belly. He goes on, not feeling the rain, the heat, or the cold. He just keeps moving, measuring the sidewalk through the cart's wire grid, swerving the wheels to avoid the curbs and holes. Like he does every day, all day long.

Yes, he walks without hearing, without seeing. Always the same. Until the arrival of one of the gray-uniformed security guards from the Secretariat of Communications and Transportation, who opens the door to the parking lot before settling behind the tollbooth window. If it's the old man with the white mustache on the day shift, he pokes him in the chest with the stick hanging off his waist. But if it's the fat red-faced guy, he kicks him in the ribs—but softly, without any intention of hurting him.

"C'mon, Vikingo, it's dawn already. Get a move on."

And, still between dreams, he asks himself who that Vikingo they're referring to could be, until, in the midst of a stomachache, cramps, and his own mind's fogginess, a distant image comes to him of a dim red mane and an unkempt beard, which he remembers seeing in a mirror or reflected on some window. *I am Vikingo.* But not before—he didn't have a beard before. But yes: Vikingo. Nobody. And so he struggles clumsily to stand up while his swollen tongue pries itself off the inside of his mouth to offer one, two, a thousand apologies.

"Sorry, chief, I didn't hear you, I swear . . ."

"You don't have to swear anything to me. Look how filthy you are today. You asshole, you probably cut yourself with a bottle, right?"

"I'm nobody. No. I didn't hear a thing."

"Look, take your damn cart and get outta here. People are gonna be coming to work soon. If the supervisor sees you, he'll probably fire me for letting a huevón like you sleep in the doorway."

That's why he's up so early, moving his feet and pushing his cart. At first, slowly, trying to ignore the swelling of his joints, the violent beating in his temples. He crosses the avenue amidst cars braking and motorists' profanities as they head downtown, and he inhales the morning smog as he nears the public square where he parades his humanity before the rushing clerks, the old women on their way home from 8 a.m. Mass at Romero de Terreros, and all the morning joggers.

Everyone turns away, some with disgust, others with fear, when they see his enormous figure dressed in multicolored pants, T-shirts, sweatshirts, sweaters, and the grease-stained coat he drags behind him. Vikingo lifts his gaze, but then covers his eyes with his hand, as if the brightness of the sun brings him bad memories. Later he slowly rounds the public square, over and over again, hoping that at the end of these turns, blackness will have settled in the skies above the city. He doesn't rest on any of the stone benches, he doesn't go near the fountain, he doesn't stroll in the garden, he doesn't walk between the trees. He never leaves the brick-colored pavement. He walks for hours to exhaust himself, to stop thinking. To get rid of the images from a life he lived many years ago. To give the neighbors time to throw something worth eating or drinking in the trash. To forget about what happens on the streets at night: what happened last night.

Something that has nothing to do with his surroundings makes him stop suddenly. He directs his focus to the treetops; the honking of the zanates reminds him of a man fleeing between shadows. The man screamed, just like those birds are doing right now. Insults could be heard. Yes. Was it yesterday? Or a different night? His memory strives to capture the data, but it's too foggy. He resumes his walk and shakes his head in denial. No, I haven't seen a thing. I swear, chief. I just walk. I don't know how to do anything else. I just walk around. I like Narvarte because it's a neighborhood with a lot of trees and birds. Nobody bothers me. I walk around the area not seeing a thing, not hearing a thing. I'm nobody. I don't even have a name.

The screeching birds distract him again. Vikingo searches the tangle of branches until he distinguishes a brown fluttering in the foliage. He smiles and steps off again. I never see anything and never hear anything. Just the birds. A step. Another. Then one more. Like that, chief. Yeah, you know, right?

The wheels of the cart squeak as if they want his attention. He reviews his load and readjusts it without slowing down. He used to carry more things: portfolios with papers from work, a wallet with IDs but no money, a ring of keys, a comb, a watch, a neck tie. That was another time, before he moved over near Parque Delta, which filled up whenever there was a baseball game with people who called him Vikingo because, according to one of the drunks, he looked a lot like a guy who played for the Diablos Rojos. When they demolished the park to build a mall, he had to look for another place to live and lost his things in the process. Or was it one of the times he was picked up by the police? He'd rather not remember.

He maneuvers to avoid two young women dressed in matching skirts and coats who carry greasy paper grocery bags. He dodges a man wearing a tie who scrapes his teeth with a toothpick. A senior citizen looking for a bench to rest. And a raucous group of teenagers sporting white shirts and pants making their way home. He goes in circles, in many circles. The soles of his feet begin to burn. A step. Another.

I don't even have a name, chief. Yes, Vikingo. That's a name? Although I did have one before. Yes. Fernando, I think. Like the boy in the photo. The one with his mother. When he was alive. Now I'm nobody.

A woman in a helmet and a blue uniform with a billy club in her hand crosses the public square just a few meters ahead of him and Vikingo is gripped with fear. He slows his steps. The image of the fleeing man reappears in his memory. No, I'm not Fernando. Fernando was that other guy. He was falling. He ran into me and the others shouted his name. I didn't see anything. I'm nobody.

He stops. His breathing is agitated. He asks himself if he has already gone this way.

A girl is standing nearby, staring right at him. She looks him up and down, from his messy red hair to the scabs on his ankles. She glances, surprised at Vikingo's hands, and moves away with a gesture of repulsion. *Yes, girl, I haven't washed,* he thinks to himself, but he immediately forgets about her to peer out across the boulevard that opens before him, a meridian full of dry palms and wide sidewalks crowded with people around the taco, tamale, cake, and juice stands. The air is loaded with dense, sweet, sticky smells. He drives the cart toward the flow and this time, yes, he clearly hears the hissing of tires and the insults. One of the drivers even opens the car door, furious as he gets out of his vehicle, but as soon as he gets a good look at the vagabond he shuts the door without saying a word.

Vikingo reaches the sidewalk across the street and pauses at a lamppost where there's a poster: *Mistreatment Meeting.* As they walk by, the men and women look at him intently. They examine his clothing with curiosity, as if they can't believe a man can wear so many things. Then they see his stained sleeves, his hands, and they quickly move away from him. He raises his face and inhales the city air: there's a strong scent of excrement and blood. A step. Another. Then one more. He walks. He pushes. Just like he pushed last night. He was Fernando. Yes. Fernando what? I'm nobody. I didn't see anything, chief, I swear. This way.

Clerks, housewives, and students chew and drink with determination, their faces reflecting pleasure and haste. They talk incessantly among themselves, joke around, laugh. Their sounds reverberate in Vikingo's eardrums. Some finish eating and light cigarettes, blowing smoke toward the sky, where the wisps join all the emanations from the cars. *They really do have a life*, says Vikingo to himself, without daring to look at them too much. They have names. Fernando or Juan or Lupe. They are somebody. Not me. I don't even have a name. The blurred memory of the previous night provokes an intense desire in him to feel tobacco smoke scraping his throat, filling his lungs. With his head down, he approaches a guy lighting a cigarette but before he can say a word, the man backs away. So Vikingo drops his head even lower and continues along. He digs inside the brown paper bag. He wants to find the smallest butt, yet comes up with one of the longest. It's stained, sticky, just like his hands. He brings it to his nose and his mouth floods with copper-flavored saliva. A step. Another. Then one more. I don't have matches.

He approaches one of the vendors, who has several cuts of meat, clusters of guts, and long sausages frying in a pot. The people eating inside the stall grow quiet when they see him. Vikingo nods, he's about to walk past when he notices an empty seat at the far end of the counter. The surface is jammed with plates of leftovers, green and red sauces, minced onion, salads, and salt shakers. Sausages hang from above, cut like flowers, as if they've been manipulated into serving as décor for the place. A guy in a dirty white apron and a cap splattered with blood strikes a block of wood with a knife; it's a rhythmic beat, almost musical. Greasy, sharp scents grow more intense, but Vikingo doesn't smell any of it, only the tobacco that still floods his nasal cavities. He parks his cart next to a garbage can and approaches the man with the apron, who smiles.

"What's up, Vikingo? You eat already? You want a taco?"

"Fernando was running . . ." the bum says while shaking his head. He holds up the hand with the cigarette. "I need a light."

"Of course, my brother. Whatever you need. Hold on a sec."

The man in the apron puts two tacos in front of Vikingo as the others watch uneasily. He lifts a box of matches from his work station, pulls one out, and lights it. Vikingo doesn't even look at the tacos. He puts the cigarette butt between his lips and leans toward the flame. He inhales. Coughs.

"Hey, what's on your hands, dude?"

Vikingo glances at the taco vendor's blood-stained apron. The hand holding the butt trembles. His knees too. He's in a hurry to get away but talks instead.

"He ran into me and I pushed him away. I don't know anything. I just walk. A step. Another. I'm nobody."

"Who ran into you?"

"He was falling . . ."

"Who?"

"I didn't see anything, chief. I don't understand. Nothing. I didn't hear anything either. I don't even have a name, although I used to. Thanks for the light. A step. Then another."

"Damn, Vikingo, you're getting worse by the day. Órale, look at yourself."

Now his heart beats faster. He breathes hard, without savoring the smoke, while gastric juices groan in his belly. I'm thirsty and I didn't see anything. Thirst. He stares at the bottle, where there's still a little something to drink, but he wants to leave it for later, because he senses he's going to need it more then. He tries to count each of his steps, each meter traversed, because the image of the running man, of Fernando, has stuck in his memory and he can't erase it. The street people and the vendors multiply on the sidewalk and he must walk slower to avoid hitting anybody with his cart. Just ahead, there's a busy metro station. He doesn't like crowds. He prefers solitude. But the streets here are only deserted at night. Vikingo looks at the sky: the sun hasn't finished its route. There's still a lot of time before dusk.

He came toward me. I didn't see anything, chief. I didn't have time to step aside. No. All I could do was move my cart. Fernando, yes. But I didn't see him. And I didn't hear him either. No. Nothing. I just walk and walk. He was falling. Bent. Holding his belly. He ran right into me and I had to push him off so I wouldn't fall. That's why my hands are dirty. There were others behind him.

When the cigarette ember almost reaches the filter, he puts his hand in the paper bag again and plucks another butt. He lights it with the dying end of the last cigarette and desperately sucks in the smoke.

There are fewer people on this block and the passersby don't look at him as much. A shoeshine boy greets him but he doesn't notice. He watches the familiar faces in the stores, behind the counters. He knows the neighborhood, the people know him too, and that calms him down. He crosses a street, turns the corner. There are fewer people each time. He finally stops in front of the church. That's where the chief is, the Big Chief, he thinks, as he stares at the cross in the bell tower and the steps that lead inside. He feels the urge to go in the temple and sit down in one of the pews alongside the old women praying. Perhaps he can find peace there. Yes, sitting in a pew in silence. He used to do it back in the day. Back when he would spend the nights around Parque Delta with others like himself. And before that. When he had a name and lived in a house with a woman and a boy.

But as soon as they form, the memories escape from his brain. He extracts yet another butt and lights it with the previous one. Yes. Fernando ran into me. I didn't see him. I didn't see the others either. No, chief, I swear it. I didn't see the plates. Or the uniforms. I didn't see anything. I didn't hear anything. I'm nobody. Not even the shots in the belly. Goodbye, Big Chief. I'll visit some other day, when it's calmer.

He takes another glance at the bell tower, at the church doors, and pushes the cart. A step. Another. Then one more.

A black cloud passing in front of the sun makes him think dusk has arrived. Vikingo has a moment of joy and sighs. He reaches for the bottle and caresses it tenderly. He doesn't open it; he'll wait to get to the government parking lot later tonight. He lifts the bottle to get a good look at it. Street liquor. How did it end up in his hands? He scratches his head and his nails run into a clump of flat and sticky hair. He smells his fingers: dirt and blood. The bottle was a gift, he remembers now. A gift from Fernando. Poor Fernando. He ran into me and fell. He was already falling. Yes. It's his blood. Poor man.

When the clouds let the sun's rays through, a mordant restlessness seizes Vikingo. He picks up his step. He walks. Pushes. I have to get to the lot entrance. I didn't see anything. The street liquor. No. The dead guy didn't give it to me, it was the others. The guys behind him, the ones who were after him. I'm nobody. I don't know anything. The street ends at another street. Vikingo looks for a sign at the corner until he sees it: *University*. The public square is there to the left. The entrance is a little further. But it's still daytime. He has to keep walking. Just like when he lived around Parque Delta. Always walking. Why? Because otherwise the guys in blue wake you up, the tecolotes, they called them. And why would they wake you up? Because that's the way it is. Because they're the law. And if they take you in, they beat you to a pulp just to amuse themselves. Better to keep walking. A step. Another. Then one more.

A woman crosses his path. She looks at him. Vikingo thinks her face looks familiar. He thinks he remembers her scolding him for being so dirty and stinking so badly, shooing him from the sidewalk, threatening to call the police if he didn't go away. He wants to go around her but the woman stops to block him. He thinks about going backward, but he can't remember how to do it; he only knows how to walk forward. The woman is so disagreeable. She comes toward him, grabs the cart, the wire grid.

"I knew you had to come this way, smelly. You're not going to get away from me. I already know what you did last night. C'mon, show me what you've got in your cart."

Last night. It wasn't me. I'm nobody. Vikingo freezes. His legs buckle. His heart races wildly. The image of this Fernando in a bloody pool flashes in his memory. Fernando. That's what the others called the guy they were after. "Fernando! Stop right there, cabrón! You want protection but you don't want to pay for it? We've come to collect, you son of a bitch!" That's what the guys in uniform were yelling at him. Then the shots. "And you, get outta the way, you fucking bum! And if you open your mouth, you know what's gonna happen to you!" The images jump to Vikingo's mind out of order, as if the woman's scolding has triggered them. Fernando running. His belly spilling blood. I pushed him and I got covered with it. Fernando on the ground. Blood on my hands. And the bottle . . . They gave me the bottle. "You haven't seen anything, you bum." "No, chief. I didn't see a thing. I never see anything. I don't hear anything. I'm nobody." "That's how we like it, cabrón. Here, take this bottle. It'll help you forget." "Yes, chief." "But we're always going to remember you. And we're the law. We can take you whenever we want. You understand?" "Yes, chief." "What's your name?" "I don't have a name, chief. I'm nobody." "Fine, I like that, now be quiet and get outta here."

"What's your name?"

"I don't have name, chief. I'm nobody."

"Don't call me chief. I'm Mrs. Chávez, the head of the neighborhood association."

"Yes, chief."

"People are complaining about the drunks and drug addicts who hang around here. I just reported you. You're the one they call Vikingo, right?"

"I'm nobody."

He tries to get her to let go of the cart, but she holds on as if she has claws. He tries again but with little success. Vikingo's bones have lost their strength, they feel like putty, watered down, drained of energy. He wants to beg the woman to let him go, to tell her he has to keep walking, but the only things out of his mouth are the same words as always.

"I didn't see anything. I didn't hear anything either. I'm nobody . . ."

"You're gonna tell me you don't know anything about the dead guy they found this morning near the government parking lot? They say there was a bum hanging around with a supermarket cart. And you're the only one around here who's always dragging a cart. Have you seen yourself? The least you could have done is washed off the blood after killing the man."

"Fernando . . ."

The woman smiles triumphantly and her face twists into a malicious mask.

"Yes, Fernando Aranda. See, you do know. Now you're gonna tell the cops everything."

"I don't know anything. I just . . ."

Desperation gives him strength to move the cart but he still can't get the woman to let go.

"You're not going anywhere, you criminal!"

"I swear, I don't know anything."

People begin to gather and listen to the argument. Some are from the neighborhood and they know both him and the woman. Others have only noticed them in passing. There's some murmuring. Vikingo recognizes words like *corpse, homicide, killer*. He remembers how, whenever there was a dead guy, the uniforms used to come for him and his friends around Parque Delta and they'd interrogate them in the bowels of the police station. He remembers the wet towels stinging his skin, the electric shocks, water spurting into his brain. Screaming in pain. The mocking questions and giving the answers over and over until he was exhausted. The answers the only words left in his brain. In his fogginess, he also remembers that before the interrogations, he knew who he was. His name. His past. A big wave of fury and panic passes through him as he distinguishes the blue and red lights from a squad car on a nearby window. The murmuring increases. *The dead*, they say. *He killed him*. He jerks the cart forcefully to loosen it and the woman screams.

"Ay! Beast! You broke my nail!"

The onlookers part as he makes his way toward them, while the woman runs in the direction of the squad car. I don't know anything, chief. I didn't see anything. I'm nobody.

Two uniformed cops get out of the car. Vikingo sees them and realizes they're the same guys who went after Fernando. Without hesitation, he grabs the liquor bottle, opens it, and drains the last bit. The alcohol makes his stomach tremble, then spreads a pleasant warmth through his body. Fernando, that was his name. They shouted his name. I didn't see anything.

"Hey, you, cabrón! Stop!"

It's the same voice from last night. They're even the same words. The only thing missing is Fernando's name. Fernando. Yes. But, unlike that guy, Vikingo doesn't run: he just walks. "I don't know anything, chief. I never see anything. I'm nobody." He recites his litany as footsteps come up behind him. He figures that history repeats itself, that they'll take him to the station's bowels, or to some other cellar, to squeeze the truth out of him, that they're going to stick him with the murder of a guy he didn't even know, like they've done so many other times, and that after a few weeks or a couple of years in the penitentiary they'll throw him back out on the streets, where he'll have to find a doorway to sleep in again and a super-market cart to keep walking. He wants another cigarette really badly. But there are no matches. "I swear, chief. That's right." When the footsteps slow down behind him, Vikingo recalls the face of the corpse from the night before. "I don't know anything. I'm nobody. I just walk. A step. Another. Then one more."

PRIVATE COLLECTION

BY Bernardo Fernández

Vallejo

T he set of jungle music Lizzy programmed on her iPod to wake her up went off at 7 in the morning. She stretched, untangling herself from the black silk sheets on the king-sized futon.

Just like every morning, the first thing she looked at when she opened her eyes was a painting by Julio Galán on the wall directly in front of the bed in her Polanco apartment.

Fifteen minutes later, her personal trainer was waiting for her in the adjoining gym with an energy drink in her hand. Helga was an ex–Olympic finalist from Germany who accompanied her everywhere.

"*Guten Tag*," said the blonde. Lizzy replied with a grunt.

Lizzy did forty minutes of aerobic exercise and an hour of weights.

At 9, after a cold shower, Lizzy ate a bowl of cereal with nonfat yogurt and drank green tea while checking her e-mail on her iPhone. Alone in the immense dining room, she peered out her large windows overlooking Chapultepec Castle. Pancho brought her breakfast from the kitchen, where he had prepared it himself.

At 10, in her office parking lot in Santa Fe, Lizzy stepped out of her car, a black 1970 Impala with flames painted on the sides.

On her orders, the car had been salvaged from a shop

in Perros Muertos, Coahuila, and sent to Los Angeles for restoration.

She busied herself during the morning hours with financial matters. Tired of the fiscal chaos left by her late father, she had sought advice from an investment counselor who suggested she diversify her portfolio.

She loved verifying her account dividends and was fascinated to see how she was getting richer every day.

At noon, she had a cold beverage, fresh fruit, a high-fiber muffin, and tea. Before lunch, at 2 in the afternoon, she took a call from a gallery in Europe. Although she'd studied at the Toronto School of Art in Canada, she'd abandoned her creative career to concentrate on building a contemporary art collection.

"Lizzy, darling, I have something that's going to blow your mind," said Thierry in his thick French accent.

"I'm not sure, Tierritas. Last time you came up with pure garbage."

"You are going to die, mon amour. I have seven pieces by David Nebrada."

After a tense silence, Lizzy asked: "How much?"

Money was never a problem.

At 2:30, she entered the VIP room at Blanc des Blancs, on Reforma, where she greeted Renato, an old industrialist friend of her father's, who was dining with the minister of labor.

The two old men invited Lizzy to join them, a proposal she gently declined before moving along to her favorite table in the back of the restaurant.

On the way, she ran into Marianito Mazo, the son of a telenovela producer, who was sitting with a couple of pop singers enjoying their fifteen minutes of fame. Marianito greeted her with a kiss, introduced the two girls, and invited her to a cocktail party he was having at his parents' house in the Pedregal the following Saturday.

"I think I'm going to be away then," said Lizzy, smiling. "Let me check and I'll have my secretary confirm it with your people."

After another warm farewell, Lizzy finally sat down. She ordered an arugula salad, salmon carpaccio, and white wine. She ate in silence while checking her e-mail on her cell. After the meal, she called her cousin Omar, who worked as a deejay at an Ibiza nightclub.

"Mademoiselle?" the waiter interrupted. "This cocktail is from the gentleman at that table."

She looked where he was pointing.

The general solicitor of the republic's private secretary winked at her from across the room.

That evening, she asked Bonnie, her secretary, to cancel all her appointments so she could get a mud-therapy treatment at a spa in Santa Fe, just a few blocks from her office.

"Don't forget that you have to go to the warehouse," noted the gringa with her clipped Texas accent.

"I won't forget, I'll go later tonight," Lizzy responded.

She decided to walk to the spa, much to Pancho's consternation; he didn't like her wandering around unprotected. But she always managed to do as she pleased.

The French girl who applied the mud for the massage, a recent arrival from Lyon, couldn't help herself and said, "You have a beautiful derriere. As firm and smooth as a peach."

"Thanks," said Lizzy.

At 8, they arrived at Tamayo Museum in her father's old

armored BMW, Pancho driving. Two light Windstar trucks packed with bodyguards followed them.

She was dressed completely in black leather, her hair pulled back in a bun speared with little chopsticks. She looked almost beautiful.

"Wait for me outside. I don't want to attract attention," she said from the door of the museum.

"Miss . . ." protested the bodyguard with the cavernous voice.

"Do as I say."

Pancho ordered the team of eight Israeli-trained escorts—two of them women—to be placed strategically in key positions around the museum. The old bodyguard monitored their movements by walkie-talkie.

The girl's whims made him nervous, but he had sworn to the Señor, her father, that he'd take care of her.

Inside, unconcerned with her bodyguards, Lizzy distributed kisses to gallery owners, art collectors, curators, critics, and artists. She was an art world celebrity. Everyone knew about her collection and her peculiar tastes. She'd surprised more than a few with her resources. No one asked where her funds came from.

The opening was for a retrospective by an Armenian-American painter named Rabo Karabekian. Eight of the pieces belonged to Lizzy's collection. As usual, she had asked that they be credited to an unnamed private collection. She didn't want any publicity.

She had to cross a human gauntlet to greet the artist, who managed to spot her even at a distance.

"Lizzy, baby!" The old artist's face lit up when he saw his favorite collector.

"How you doing, Rab?"

They chatted animatedly for half an hour. When the press wanted to take photos, Lizzy demurred.

The painter told her that there would be an after-party at the curator's apartment in Condesa, that he would love it if she came by. She apologized.

"Got some business to take care of, sorry," and she said goodbye to everyone.

On the way to the car, her cell rang.

"Got 'em," growled a voice on the other end of the line.

Seconds of silence.

"You have them with you?"

"Correct."

"I'm going to give you a kiss on the nose, like Scooby-Doo," Lizzy said before hanging up.

She got in the BMW and asked to be taken to the warehouse.

Pancho silently directed the car toward the warehouse that MDA, their ghost company, had leased in an industrial park in Vallejo. They did not exchange a word during the trip.

The security team at the warehouse waved them in, surprised by the late hour of the visit. A heavy steel door slid open to let the BMW and the Windstars pass.

Bwana, Lizzy's lieutenant on the north side of the city, received them. He was a cholo, an ex–juvenile delinquent who had learned something about chemistry during his years as a science student. A violent type, he had been raised on the streets of East L.A.

Secretly, Lizzy found him attractive and was fascinated by the wild beauty of his indigenous features; his athletic body, always clothed in baggy jeans, was like a basketball player's; his naked torso was covered with tattoos of the Virgin of

Guadalupe and Santa Muerte; his nipples sported rings.

Sometimes, in her deepest dreams, Lizzy allowed herself fantasies about the muscle-bound cholo. Fantasies that vanished as soon as she woke up.

"What's up, boss?" said Bwana in greeting just outside the warehouse. He had a .38 sticking out of his pants and a green bandanna covering his shaved head.

"I want this over with. Where they are?"

"This way," he said as he entered the warehouse. Lizzy followed, leaving behind her escorts and the warehouse security guards.

Bwana guided her through narrow corridors of boxes labeled with Korean characters. Pancho walked behind them, a few meters back, with a canvas backpack on his shoulder that caught Bwana's attention.

Lizzy had specified that the walkways be designed like a labyrinth. Only a few people knew the way to the center. The architect, a gay old maid who used to walk his dogs on Amsterdam Avenue, had been found dead on the freeway to Toluca after he'd finished the job.

The cholo was saying something to his boss but she found it impossible to understand because of the rapid mix of Spanglish and border slang. Every time they reached a door, Bwana keyed an access code into the electronic lock that protected the crossing.

When they arrived at the center of the warehouse, Bwana entered another code. This time, a trapdoor opened, revealing stairs that led to an underground chamber; these were covered by a layer of high-density foam rubber, just like a recording studio.

Moans could be heard coming from below. Barely audible, more like murmurs.

"Welcome to special affairs, boss," said Bwana.

Lizzy descended the steps. The basement was dark. A switch was touched and a light went on, revealing where the sounds were coming from.

A man and a woman were tied with barbed wire to vinyl chairs and gagged with cinnamon-colored gaffer tape. The woman had a ruptured eye. They were covered with dry blood, a pool of excrement gathered at their feet.

"They stink," mumbled Lizzy.

Pancho obediently sprayed both bodies with the Lysol he carried in the canvas backpack. The man and woman twisted from the sting of the aerosol.

Lizzy approached the woman and looked with curiosity at her ruined eye.

"You said she was with him when they got him?"

"Correct. She's his bitch. Bad luck."

The Constanza cartel boss turned toward the bound man.

It was Wilmer, assistant to Iménez, the Colombian capo with whom Lizzy had been negotiating just weeks before. Bwana's people had discovered they were bringing Brazilian amphetamines on their own into the country.

Bad idea.

Wilmer had been the person in charge of the operation. Then, he was a real mean motherfucker. Now, what was left of him whimpered like a kicked puppy.

Lizzy noticed a tear sliding down his filthy cheek.

"Deep in shit, everybody's the same."

Then she kicked the man's jaw aikido-style. She felt the bone crack under her foot. The blow knocked him to the ground. His scream would have echoed in the chamber had it not been soundproofed.

The woman began to struggle, trying to shout from under the tape sealing her cracked lips.

Lizzy tore the tape off in one quick move. In the process, she also tore off a good bit of skin.

"What did you say?"

"Please . . . pu . . . pu-leeze . . . you . . . I have . . . a daughter . . ."

On the ground, the man sobbed. Lizzy flipped him over with the tip of her boot. *"Cry like a woman for what you couldn't defend as man,"* she said, then reached her hand out to Pancho.

The bodyguard removed a wooden bat with a Mazatlán Deers logo from the canvas backpack; it had a dozen four-inch steel nails sticking out of it. Lizzy had inherited it from her father.

"*We* deal with amphetamines here," she said to the man on the ground, "and I don't like sudacas who get in the way. This is what happens to anybody who tries to horn in on my market. Consider this a declaration of war."

She advanced toward the man with the bat in her hand. Pancho was silently thankful to have only one eye and to have the scene play out on his blind side. Discreetly, Bwana turned his gaze to the door.

When the woman in the chair saw what was about to happen, she began to scream uncontrollably.

THE CORNER

BY PACO IGNACIO TAIBO II

Doctores

D on't even think you're making me happy, okay? Don't even think it. Don't say a word, just shut up, puto. Don't even open your fucking mouth or I'll shut it myself . . . Everything is your fucking fault."

The last two words didn't actually come out like that, but more like "foshin foolt," because of all the blood in his mouth. Then he spit, half vomiting, half choking. And then he died. Of course he had to die like that, like a pendejo, trying to blame somebody else.

Agent Manterola approached the dead guy and took his car keys, his wallet, and the pair of very big, very dark sunglasses off his head that made him look like a Mayan mummy. Then, after thinking about it, he dropped them back on the ground near the body. Manterola grabbed the guy's nose and pulled on it. Dead guys aren't so scary. He took off one of the guy's shoes, just for the hell of it, and put it on his belly. He didn't even glance at the other body, that stupid fucking corpse, because it had been that one's fault that the whole mess started in the first place.

Now it was the fault of the fucking pins with the multicolored heads. *Fucking diaper pins*, Manterola muttered to himself. And he was right. Modernity had arrived at the Office of Urban Crimes, but only in the form of two old computers, though they had somehow managed to get their hands on a huge map of Mexico City, where they marked crime scenes with the multicolored pins. Red for murder, pink for sex crimes, yellow for altercations, green for assaults, blue for kidnappings, lavender for robberies in taxis, orange for carjackings. The Boss of Bosses had passed through the office earlier in the day and had been furious when he saw that that fucking corner couldn't take one more fucking pin.

So when Manterola got to work, with his funeral suit on—in other words, the same old gray suit he wore every day—with new huevos a la Mexicana stains on the lapels and a black band on his sleeve, he wasn't surprised to find the commander there staring at the map, waiting for him.

And he wasn't surprised by what he said either: "What do you think I, the commander, or the chief, or the head of government, thinks when he sees that fucking corner can't take one more fucking pin?"

Manterola knew he was going to have to pay for not taking better care of his partner, for letting him go ahead on the raid where he ran into that wacko with the machete in his hand.

"What do you want me to do, boss?"

"You tell me. And whatever it is, do it alone. I'm not assigning you a partner because they always get killed. But whatever you're going to do, just do it. Silvita will deal with the paperwork."

Manterola gazed over at the map with the intensity of a Japanese tourist standing in front of the Mona Lisa at the Louvre.

The cursed corner, focus of everything. The intersection of Doctor Erasmo and Doctor Monteverde in a neighborhood of doctors, just two blocks from the Viaduct. A lower-middle-class neighborhood which had turned destitute and disenfranchised during the crisis in the '70s, when auto-repair shops became stolen auto-parts dealers.

There was no glamour here. It was a symbol of sleazy and desperate times. It had no relation to the great criminal corners, like the one behind Santa Veracruz in the '50s, or Loneliness Square, where a homeless death-squad drank industrial-strength alcohol until they dropped, where it was said they'd steal your socks without touching your shoes. It had no relation to the edge of Ixtapalapa, very near Neza, where the Mexican state police committed their crimes in the '80s. It was the kind of place that Leone would have filmed one of his Westerns.

So for the novelist José Daniel Fierro, the call from the top dog in Mexico City's government wasn't a good thing, no matter how unusual it was, in spite of the fact that the only things he liked lately were unusual.

"Fierro, what can we do with Mexico City's worst corner, the most dangerous one, the one with the most crimes?"

"Give it to Los Angeles. Aren't we sister cities or something like that? Hollywood would love it." José Daniel heard a chuckle on the other end of the line, then tried a couple of other proposals. "You could move there, rent an apartment. With your bodyguards you'd scare them off to the next corner . . . Or send all the cops on vacation to Acapulco and then watch the crime rate come down."

This time the chuckle wasn't as hearty.

"I'm serious," said the government official. José Daniel had known Germán Núñez for years, since the dark days of the PRI when they'd been beaten up together at a political demonstration. He'd had his right eyebrow sliced by a blade and Germán had been kicked in the nuts so hard he'd had to stay in bed for a week putting up with his friends' jokes.

"And you called a novelist for this?"

"Exactly. A writer of detective fiction. I'm sending you a dossier with a bike messenger. You're going to love this story."

José Daniel Fierro, novelist, and Vicente Manterola, cop, analyzed the cursed corner for the reasons already stated. But they didn't have the same data. Fierro reviewed a study with a statistical appendix. Manterola had a pile of files that went back a couple of years. Perhaps because they were notably different people, from different cities, with different skeletons in their closets and disparate personal histories, they reached different conclusions.

"If I could fuck with two of these gangs of car thieves, I could take down half the damn robbery pins, easy, and maybe some of the assault ones, because when they don't have cars to steal, that's what they do, and maybe even some of the yellow pins too, because half the time they're fighting each other," Manterola said in a low voice to the head of the Ezcurdia squad, who stared at him with no love lost, since one of those gangs gave him a cut so that he'd always make himself scarce.

"If you fuck with one gang, I'll tell the other to go steal someplace else, to go rip off cars in Toluca for a month," the squad leader said in response. "I don't want any problems with the head of government."

"Let's have a festival on that corner, a cultural festival," José Daniel suggested to the head of government.

"Do you want some meat, my royal sir?"

"If I want meat, I'll go to the supermarket, pendeja," Manterola said to a transvestite, whose real name was undoubtedly something like Manolo—or Luis Jorge or Samuel Eduardo, because now, thanks to those fucking Venezuelan telenovelas, it had become fashionable to give babies two names. The guy didn't actually look too bad: nice legs, even nicer ass, and no question that if he'd run into him in the dark, he'd have given him a whirl.

Manterola knew all too well that more than one of his colleagues liked to be with queens, but always with their macho thing of who-fucked-who. If you did the fucking, you weren't the fag in the picture. The puto was the other guy. Lord have mercy, what assholes his colleagues could be. Like the dude who said he was disgusted by the whole thing but that his body "asked for it" sometimes.

It was getting dark. To get rid of the faggot, Manterola just ignored him and leaned up against a lamppost at the corner of Doctor Erasmo and Doctor Monteverde, right in front of a grocery store called La Flor de Gijón which shone its neon through a swarm of flies. He watched the movements inside for a while: maids buying bread, two kids who went in for soda carrying a huge plastic bag. An s.o.b. with the face of an s.o.b. buying cigarettes. Some dude, Cuban or coastal—impossible to tell the difference in the dark—mouthing a cumbia and lazily picking up a six-pack of beer. The old man at the register looked like he'd opened the store after being left back from Cortés's first expedition. Having absorbed all of this, Manterola entered.

"Good evening."

"Fuck, that's the first time in my life a cop has greeted me with a *good evening*," said the old man—pale like a Spaniard—with a toothless smile.

"How many times have you been robbed?"

"None so far," replied the old man, with an expression that made it clear he expected nothing good to come from a police visit.

"Even though you're on the most dangerous corner in all of Mexico City," said Manterola.

"What do you mean?"

"You're gonna gimme that story too?"

"Who else told you that?"

"A writer."

There's going to be a cultural event of some sort on your corner. It's a kind of party, a festival, but sponsored by the government. You have to speak with a man whose last name is Mechupas, said the note scribbled on the Post-it on his desk. Manterola put his hands on his head and discovered his hair was wet with sweat. He'd never heard of such a thing.

He put his files in order, with the one for Fermín Huerta on top. That was the guy, El Mandarín. That was his Saint Peter at the gates of heaven. But what the fuck was this about a party?

Mechupas was obviously the writer José Daniel Fierro.

"Well, my esteemed officer, if you don't like it, you can call Mexico City's head of government yourself," he said, offering a worn business card. "Here's his number."

Manterola eyed the Boss of Bosses' business card and read the message on it: *This is the information we discussed.*

Later, he checked in again on the novelist. He was a big guy, with a mustache like Pancho Villa; it was probably best to just be straight with him.

José Daniel, who knew a lot about shady characters, saw

the doubt in the cop's small eyes right away. *Let's see if this guy learns to respect those of us who don't wear ties,* he said to himself.

Let's see if I can learn to respect people who don't wear ties, Manterola said to himself at that same moment, *even if they're a bunch of lazy pendejos.*

"So?"

"We're going to have a festival, and you're not going to arrest anybody, nor raid anything, nor insult anybody, nor shoot anybody, nor bother anybody, nor fuck with anybody on that corner, which I understand is under your jurisdiction."

"Señor Fierro, we have a very important investigation underway," Manterola said ceremoniously.

"Well, you can shove it up your ass," said Fierro, who wasn't much liked by the state police anyway, and who was seeing red because Manterola had come into his life asking what the fuck he was thinking throwing a party on his corner.

"So what is my role here then?"

"Work with me. And if you have any questions, call the head of government, or your boss, or the Boss of Bosses," said Fierro while lighting a delicate filtered cigarette and smiling.

Manterola surrendered for the moment. "What do you want me to do?"

"Help me find El Mandarín," said Fierro, who'd done his homework.

He was called El Mandarín, not just because he was Chinese but also because he had dyed a red streak in his hair that made him look like a peeled mandarin orange. Manterola knew he wasn't a car thief; the guy was a middle manager in the acquisitions department of a large and growing enterprise that included various parking lots, a half dozen garages, about a hundred employees, an office with multiple bookkeepers, connections with public officials in three different states who supplied fake papers, a customs chief in Veracruz and another in Coatzacoalcos, and even space on various marine freighters. What he did wasn't even a crime—a crime is stealing from old women, beating up your wife, kicking a baby—this was business. El Mandarín knew that if all the cars stolen in one year in the Valley of Mexico were lined up, they would reach Cuernavaca, more than seventy kilometers away. That was why it was great business.

El Mandarín was eighteen years old, the senior member of his gang, which was an immense responsibility, so he didn't steal cars on Tuesdays or Thursdays because he was too busy studying Russian. He'd heard a few things: that Volkswagens sold well in North Africa because they were air-cooled instead of water-cooled; that small trucks did well in Guatemala; and that Dodge was all the rage in Eastern Europe, where everybody spoke Russian.

Manterola and José Daniel found him at the entrance to his high school and he made no move to run. It would have been different in his own neighborhood, but he had no idea where he could run around here.

"I guess I'm fucked," he said, and resigned himself to a simple smile.

You only go back at night when you want something. I return to the dark so that it'll keep me from the day's perverse routines, from the failures of love. José Daniel Fierro was writing on his keyboard when the doorbell got stuck. He bitched all the way to the door because one of his legs had fallen asleep. It was 4 in the morning.

Manterola measured him with a killer gaze.

"You want to have a charanga or a chimichurri or a chimiganga or whatever the fuck you call it—a masked ball on that corner? That's all we need—you let them wear masks while they rob us, you give all those assholes an excuse to dress up as wrestlers so they can fuck with us."

Fierro sighed and pulled out a cigarette.

The festival was one of the biggest successes in the history of the Neighborhood of Doctors. Years later people would still be talking about how well Tania Libertad sang, how delicious the carnitas were, how beautifully the kids read their poetry, and especially about the endless conga started by El Mastuerzo when he screamed out, "Viva Emiliano Zapata!"

There were no problems with the police. Community members stopped two domestic disturbances, kept kids from drinking beer, and even caught a bike thief who'd come over from Buenos Aires.

José Daniel Fierro gave the corner a leading role in the last few chapters of his novel; he even violated his own literary sensibilities and ended the story with an over-the-top kitschy description of two teens kissing at dusk at the intersection of Doctor Erasmo and Doctor Monteverde.

Agent Vicente Manterola was arrested in Puebla for raping a queen who was friendly with the local governor. While he was detained, a prisoner who didn't like how Manterola was looking at him took one of his eyes out with a scrap from an empty soda can.

El Mandarín ended up in North Africa, driving a gypsy cab in Casablanca.

The corner was no longer cursed after the festival. The multicolored pins moved malevolently to other corners of Mexico City.

The owner of the Flor de Gijón retired and, since he'd saved a small fortune, went to live in the country of his birth. The day he left Mexico, he nearly bumped into José Daniel Fierro at the airport, but the writer didn't recognize him since he was too busy buying duty-free cigarettes.

THE UNSMILING COMEDIAN
BY F.G. Haghenbeck
Condesa

I heard Andrea Rojas's name the same day I met Cantinflas. She was nice, smart, and had a fine sense of humor.
Not Cantinflas. He was like the other stars at Cinelandia:
simply a star.

While President Lyndon B. Johnson prepared to send a
man to the moon, I decided to stay for a couple of months
in Mexico City. I wanted to do pretty typical things: go to a
wrestling match; bet on the bull in a bullfight at Plaza Mexico;
drink a bottle of tequila at a bar in Tenampa; and enjoy a ba-
nana split at the Roxy. I also wanted to do an atypical thing:
take care of my mother while she recovered from surgery. Her
convalescence had yanked me out of my half-life as a beatnik
bloodhound in Venice Beach. Nothing mattered much to me.
Anyway, it's always pleasant to spend time in the place where
I was born. But not a lot of time, because the city is a treacher-
ous lover. Those who love and live here only deal in pain.

Knowing that I was hanging out on my old turf, my ex-
boss recommended me for a local job. Ever since he'd retired,
he parceled out work like Santa Claus. I supposed I'd been
good that year: it brought me Cantinflas.

The interview was outside the city, in a luxurious subdivision called Jardines del Pedregal de San Ángel, nestled in
volcanic rock from an eruption as ancient as my Ford Woody.
The house was great. It looked like a giant concrete sandwich

with huge windows and austere furniture. The view was glorious; snow-covered volcanoes could be seen through a cactus garden.

I was led to the waiting room. I think it had higher aspirations than just to *wait*. It could have been a soccer field or a national stadium. I sat in a chair next to several trophies. After reading the plaque on a statuette that said Fortino Mario Alfonso Moreno Reyes, a.k.a. "Cantinflas," had won the Golden Globe, I got bored. But a loud voice soon stirred me from my reverie.

"I was told you're good. But I'd like references, Mr. Sunny Pascal." The voice came from behind a door and then the comedian entered. I found myself before Mexico's most successful actor. He wasn't much taller than me. That was something. (In Los Angeles, I was considered Snow White's lost dwarf.) He was dressed in a loud wine-colored chamois jacket. White turtleneck and dark glasses as big as a windshield. He walked slowly. Carefully. As he got closer, I noticed he must have been about fifty years old, but that recent cosmetic surgery made him seem forty or so. He still had some bandages. His prim face had the look of money: gringo dollars.

"I know you've won a lot of awards but, to me, that doesn't make you an actor," I responded. My insolence was gratuitous. He didn't say anything. Instead, there was a pause that hung in the space between us.

"I suppose you'll need to be paid in dollars," he pressed me as he sat down in one of the chairs. Somewhere in Denmark, somebody was surely opening a champagne bottle because Cantinflas had bought one of their designs.

"Just like you got paid for *Around the World in Eighty Days* and *Pepe*," I answered even more insolently. He didn't smile. He didn't have much of a sense of humor for a comedian.

"Those films were failures. The gringos don't understand my common man's sense of humor. Here in Mexico I'm king," he explained, as he opened a silver case and extracted a cigarette. He offered me one. I declined. I didn't want to be a walking cliché. I'm the only detective I know who doesn't smoke. "I will pay for your silence. Carmandy assures me you're the type who can keep his mouth shut. That's important because of my reputation."

"You can trust me. In fact, I knew Doris Day when she was a virgin." I gave him my most ingenuous smile. He didn't so much as blink. He was certainly greedy with his humor. He saved it all up for the camera.

"I've received some letters. They want money . . . a lot of money. They say they have information that could hurt me," he told me as he smoked. It was impossible to see his eyes behind the shades. I was starting to feel uncomfortable.

"Is it true?"

"That's none of your business. You just follow orders," he grunted. I stood up. I straightened my black guayabera and turned toward the door. He made a gesture with his hand to stop, so I sat back down. "I'm sorry. I'm used to the barbarians who run this city's police department."

"Exactly what do you want me to do, Mr. Moreno?" I asked, trying to sound professional. The beatnik beard and my huaraches weren't helping.

"Andrea Rojas. Pay her off. Tell her it's the only time I'll pay for her silence. The press and the police have already cleared me of any wrongdoing in Myriam's death," he groused. He said her name as if he'd stepped in dog shit. Through his dark glasses, he could see from the expression on my face that I didn't know what he was talking about. "Myriam Roberts, an American model. She killed herself at the Alfer Hotel a couple of years ago. She left a suicide note for me."

Cantinflas took a piece of paper from his jacket and handed it to me. It was a simple note written in a fine feminine script. It could have been a love letter or a grocery list.

Dear Mario,
Please forget me. You could never love me and I could never understand this place. Be good to yourself. You have been good to me but you could never love me, yet I really loved you. I know you'll be good to our son.

When I finished reading the letter, I gave it back to him. He folded it carefully and put it back in his jacket pocket, the one over his heart.

"Are you going to tell me the whole story or just the condensed *Reader's Digest* version?"

The comedian shrugged his shoulders. "The police questioned me. I'd known her for many years. The boy's name is Carlos. I adopted him, he's my son now. I don't want her to continue threatening my family. Find Rojas, pay her off, and make sure she never bothers me again."

At the door, a secretary appeared, more stacked than the pyramids at Teotihuacán. Her miniskirt barely contained her, and her beehive practically hit the ceiling. She gave me a bundle of dollars and a letter, assuring my silence.

"Even if you don't take the job, you'll have to sign the confidentiality agreement. I don't want you to sell the story about my cosmetic surgery to Mike Oliver for three tequilas, and I don't want this house surrounded by bloodsucking photographers."

"I accept. Don't worry. Carmandy is right, I'm a lot cuter

when I'm quiet." I pocketed the dollars and signed the agreement. We Mexicans are proud. We don't like to air our dirty laundry. We don't like it when the rest of the world finds out we have bad breath.

In the mid-'60s, Mexico City was dressed up and made to look like a fashionable urban center. President López Mateos built a Los Angeles–style highway, to which he gave the flirty name, El Periferico. The city delighted in the contrasts between modern buildings, colonial constructions, and rustic homes. It was sprinkled with cabarets, from the finest like the Source and the Casino Terrace, to the Fifth Patio and the Empire. My love of cocktails had free rein at all of them.

I left the comedian's house with the bundle of bills and an address to make the delivery. I hid the cash in the secret compartment where I usually stashed the Colt. Such an absence of humor had made me thirsty. My mouth was begging for a drink even though it wasn't yet noon. I drove my Ford Woody through streets with names lifted from a Walt Whitman poem: Rock, Water, Fountains, Rain, Breeze, Clouds. I was mentally composing my own poem when I noticed that an enormous cobalt-blue Lincoln Continental was following me. It was as imposing as a pirate ship. The car cut me off, forcing me to stop, and out stepped a huge brown dude who looked like a miniature King Kong.

"Who the fuck do you think you are to stick your nose in our business, pendejo?" He spit on my windshield. King Kong Jr. wore an absurdly wide pink tie that carried evidence of his breakfast. The suit was actually a couple of sizes too small. But what I disliked most was that he stunk of garlic.

"It's been a long time since I thought I was much of anybody, bud," I calmly answered. But it was a mistake. I knew it when I saw his fist come through the window like a medieval battering ram. The impact practically knocked me out of the car. I would have trouble breathing through my nose that night.

The friendly gorilla hit me two more times. Once I was out of the car and on the ground, he gave me two kicks, which I can still feel. When there was enough blood on the pavement, he went through my pockets.

"Who brought you in, cabrón? It was that asshole Rojas, right?" He repeated his questions as he went through my papers. He took his time. I don't think he'd ever finished elementary school. He gave them back to me with a grunt. "A maricón gringo detective! That's all we need!"

He checked out my car; he went through everything. I watched him toss out my Los Castros record, a bra whose owner I couldn't remember, and an empty bottle of tequila.

"Where's the money?" he asked. Just so I understood him properly, he made his point by kicking me again.

"I have three dollars and twenty pesos in my wallet," I blathered.

The gorilla bent down until we were almost face-to-face. If I'd been a romantic guy, I might have kissed him. But he wasn't my type: blond and curvy.

"You fuck with me and I kill you. Do you understand me, gringuito?"

"I'm Mexican," I managed to say. But he didn't hear me. He took my dollars and left. It took a good while for me to get up. I don't use a watch so I had to depend on my bladder. When the need to pee became greater than the pain, that's when I made my move. The street was still empty. All I could see were the big doors on the mansions. I unzipped and began to unload my bladder. I had barely started when I heard a po-

lice siren. They're never there when you need them. But they
fined me on a morals charge.

I recuperated with five tequilas. There might have been more.
I slept for two days straight and, when I got bored with the
game shows on TV, I went back to work. I checked out the
address on the paper the secretary had given me. It was in
the Condesa neighborhood, just a few steps from the Roxy
ice-cream parlor. I drove to an apartment building in front of
a beautiful park with big trees and a duck pond. There were
Orthodox Jewish mothers in the park with their baby stroll-
ers and old Spanish Republicans too, smoking aromatic cigars
and still dreaming of killing Franco. It was an island in the
city's chaos. A sigh for immigrants.

There was a bike repair shop next to the side door of the
building. They were also for rent, those machines which cause
only pain and tears. An employee was reading *La Prensa* while
eating tamales.

"Good afternoon, how you doing?" I asked as if I had
nothing better to do.

"Bad, but it'll get better when school lets out," the bike
mechanic said without a pause in his sacred lunch. In Mexico City, the lunch hour is blindly respected. Even if there
were a war between Soviet and American missiles, everybody would still go out for lunch and get something greasy
and spicy.

"I'm looking for a friend. She lives in this building. Maybe
you know her: Andrea Rojas."

"Miss Rojas? She lives in apartment 202. She's sleeping,"
he said, still chewing.

"Must have been quite a night. Drinks, partying . . ."

The guy opened his eyes wide as tortillas and laughed.

"No time for that! Don't you know she's in school and works too? She was drawing the whole night, doing her homework. I got her dinner so she wouldn't lose any time."

I must have looked like an idiot. My inkling had been a bust.

"I better not wake her then," I said as I left. The mechanic continued eating.

I bought some ice cream, pistachio. I played lookout from one of the park benches. Andrea Rojas emerged a couple of hours later, after a herd of kids had rented some bikes and entertained themselves by leaving pieces of their knees all over the pavement.

She left the building and waved at the mechanic. He said something to her and pointed at me. Andrea Rojas turned toward me; I could see her better. Well, it sure was a pleasure to look at her. Her hair was black, very dark. Pine nut–colored skin highlighted her eyes. A slender but firm body. Every curve was where it should be. Dressed in a miniskirt, wearing black stockings. She also wore a beret tilted slightly to the left. She was a goddess, beautiful and hip.

"I don't remember having you as a friend. But you're not a cop: you're too short and too shabby. Who are you?" she asked, her hands on her hips.

I considered responding right away, but decided to take my time so I could enjoy her. "I'm a friend of a friend."

"This mutual friend, does he have a name or did his parents not have enough money to baptize him?" She was quick. She'd be a hard bone to chew.

"Moreno. Some call him Mario. Some don't."

Her deep black eyes stabbed me like a pair of knives and she cursed under her breath. "Tell him to quit fucking with me!" she barked.

I got up from the park bench and followed her. I had to hurry; she was fast.

"Funny you should say that. He said the exact same thing."

Andrea Rojas turned around in disgust. She raised her shoulders and screamed, "I've already told him it isn't me! I didn't send that note—" But before she could finish scolding me, I noticed the cobalt-blue Lincoln approaching us. I immediately threw the girl to the ground. The bullets whizzed right above our heads. By the time I got up, the car had vanished. Andrea remained on the ground. I liked that she didn't cry. I'm attracted to strong women.

"We need to talk. And you have no idea how badly I need a drink."

"Motherfucker, I need two," she said, her face white as a ghost.

I almost proposed on the spot.

We walked a few blocks, slowly entering the trendy new neighborhood where bars, restaurants, and shops vied to trap unwitting tourists: the Zona Rosa. We followed my nose for cocktails and chose a tiki bar named the Mauna Loa. I told her who I was, what I did, and I told her about my life. That took about twenty minutes. When it was her turn, she talked for more than two hours. I didn't care: a mai tai accompanied by those black eyes was pretty close to paradise.

She told me she studied architecture at the university. In her free time, she worked as a nanny and belonged to a student group that liked to talk politics, smoke pot, and fix the country with their ideas. That's where she'd met her boyfriend. His parents were dead and his only kin was an uncle who lived in Guatemala. She was independent, exciting, and beautiful. I'd just landed the top prize.

". . . young people should come together, the future is in our hands," she said excitedly.

"I don't see how I could change the world. I'd need to be Superman and put on that cape to defend justice. So long as I don't have superstrength and the power to fly, I think I'll stick with surviving," I confessed. It was pretty low-grade philosophy, but it was mine, and I wasn't just going to give it away either.

"Maybe that's what you should do: be a superhero and save the needy, not work for the oppressors," she scolded. She was even more attractive when angry.

"Like your old boss, Mr. Moreno? Is that why you blackmailed him?" I went at her hard. I didn't need to be that cruel but I had to earn my money.

"He only hired me to take care of his son. He was married to another woman and didn't know what to do. I helped him with the boy after the suicide," she said offhandedly.

"And there wasn't an extracurricular relationship? He's pretty famous."

"You think I was involved with Mr. Moreno? You're a pervert!" she said, but she was laughing at me. My case was falling apart. She wasn't blackmailing him. "He paid for the funeral and the services when Miss Myriam died. I don't know if he loved her but he kept his promise to take care of the boy without letting the scandal affect his wife. Even so, the police always tried to implicate him."

"The police?"

"Yeah, those guys with the shields, the guns, and faces like dogs. If you don't know them, I'll gladly introduce you." She sipped her drink with a sly grin and let herself be contemplated. She knew I was caught in her web. "And you? Do you have a woman?"

"Not that I know of," I blurted, thrown off by the question.

"Do you have a man?" she shot at me. She was getting her revenge.

"No, I don't have anyone or anything—animal, vegetable, or mineral. What about *your* boyfriend?"

"That's in the past. He studied philosophy and letters. He loved social causes more than me. That's why I left him."

"Wow, a real Superman. Did he use that old trick with the eyeglasses to make himself appear as a nerd? I can do that even without the eyeglasses."

She didn't respond. Instead, she made a face—half smile, half disgust. After a moment, she said, "I'm not the person who sent those notes to Mr. Moreno. Anyway, it's been nice. I need to get home. Pancho Villa hasn't eaten." She put her beret back on.

"The guy in the blue car could be waiting for you. It won't be good for your health," I said. That didn't stop her. She was a rock.

"Well, I'd have to go back someday. If they want to hurt me, I can't stop them."

"Let me go with you. I could be your hero . . ." I mumbled as I dropped a couple of bills to cover the drinks. I followed her to the door. "Pancho Villa?"

"My black cat," she said in a schoolgirl's voice. I melted.

By the time we got to her building, the kids who'd rented the bikes were gone, probably drinking hot chocolate at home. Nighttime gave the neighborhood a different air, refreshing it with the sound of families murmuring around their TVs. The mechanic was still at the shop. He'd replaced the tamales with a bottle of beer, some tacos, and a buddy.

He waved when he saw us. While Andrea searched her

bag for her keys, I saw an enormous black cat at the window-sill. I figured it was General Villa and smiled at him.

As soon as Andrea opened the front door to the building, my nose was assaulted by a strong garlic smell. I recognized it. I knew it was emanating from an orangutan wearing a wide tie. When I tried to stop Andrea, King Kong Jr. leaped from a corner, gun in hand. He threw his arm around the girl's neck like a snake. I cursed myself for having left the Colt in the car.

"I told you to keep out of this, gringuito," the guy grunted.

Andrea didn't even try to make a move. She knew this man wouldn't hesitate to shoot her.

"I know he gave you money to give to her. But this is my doing. She doesn't have a clue what's going on. You shouldn't have interfered, you asshole," he sneered. Andrea didn't seem surprised.

"You're the cop in charge of Miss Myriam's case," she deciphered. The gorilla twitched unhappily, but didn't let go. For an instant, he looked upset about being fingered. Then he went back to what he knew best: being a motherfucker.

"Shut the the fuck up, you fucking hag! And you, where's the cash?"

I raised my arms. I was at the threshold of the building entrance. "It's in my car."

"Don't lie to me or I'll kill her!" he screamed.

I raised my arms even higher. "It's hidden in the place I normally stash my gun. That's why you didn't find it last time," I explained. He turned to look at Andrea. Ever the rock, she just stared back at him with her black eyes, attacking him for having involved her in something so unseemly.

"Let's go. Don't pull any shit."

We moved toward the street. I walked slowly. The bike

mechanic and his buddy were in the midst of their partying. If we made it to the car, trying to take off with the money would surely get us both killed. I quickly glanced around, then lifted one of the bikes and threw it with all my might at King Kong Jr. He wasn't expecting it. He let go of Andrea to aim his gun. The bike hit his hand and knocked the weapon toward him, but his finger was still on the trigger. The bullet crossed his eyes. Just like in the movies, the gorilla dropped dead to the ground. There was no blonde to cry for him. The mechanic got up and approached the body. "Hijo de la chingada!"

"It's fucking good." I brought the cup to my lips and slurped the margarita, then put it back on the silver tray. I looked around. The place was beautiful. We were in a colonial hacienda, on the patio, serenaded by chirping birds and a gurgling fountain. A waiter, as discreet as an obstetrician, had just brought our drinks. Cantinflas had his own assistant on hand. It looked as if the newly opened restaurant at the San Ángel Inn was the place to be. All of its patrons seemed to work in the movies, TV, politics, or had at least been involved in sex scandals.

I removed the bundle of dollars from my pants pocket and put it on the table next to my drink. Mr. Moreno stared down at the bills for a second, then they disappeared into his mustard-colored jacket.

"I took my fee from the money. I hope there's no problem with that," I told him as I drank the wonderful elixir.

"Then you can guarantee that I'll never be bothered by that blackmail attempt again? I'm surprised you don't need the money . . ." he said with a funny smile; he had erased all traces of his surgery for this public appearance.

"I guarantee it. That's not your problem anymore. I recommend you find another one," I responded, finishing off my drink. It was a fact: the San Ángel Inn was the best place for a margarita.

"How do I know you're telling me the truth, Mr. Pascal?"

"The same way I thought you were telling me the truth when you hired me. And, actually, you lied that time." I moved a little closer to him. He didn't budge. He rested on the stool with his legs crossed. "You neither told me you'd hired an ex–police officer to pay the blackmail, nor that when they asked for more money, you fired him because you wanted it to go away. You also never told me it was the same cop who'd interrogated you about the suicide."

I waited for a reaction from the movie star. He really did deserve a Golden Globe. He didn't even arch an eyebrow.

"I owe you an apology," he said, as if he'd merely bumped into me.

I shook my head, disgusted, and got up. A waiter showed me the bill for the margaritas I'd been drinking. I passed it to the famous comedian.

"My pay includes expenses," I said. The curtain had fallen. I was in the way now. I wanted to leave the terrace but found I couldn't. I had to know the truth. "I keep asking myself if you knew that cop was the person blackmailing you in Andrea's name. Maybe you hired him to protect her. Maybe you feared he'd hurt her. You wanted to save her. You wanted me to kick his ass and you'd come out of it squeaky-clean. Was that it?"

In an instant, he put in play the simpleton character that he'd had such success with in his movies. His voice changed, he moved differently. In other words, he ceased being Mario Moreno and became Cantinflas.

"That's the thing, chato. I'm not the one to tell it, and you aren't the one to hear it, but rest assured that it'd be pretty tough to figure out . . ."

He left me with a great big smile. The only one he ever gave me.

Andrea Rojas was waiting for me outside. She was watching the construction on the corner: a Polish factory being converted into housing units. It was being painted in loud colors: blue, yellow, and red.

"Diego Rivera and Frida Kahlo used to live there," she told me. "Each one had their own apartment but he had a bridge built over to her bedroom, since he lived on the other side. Isn't that romantic?"

"I would have made the bed bigger. It's a cheaper solution." I was a little drunk from the margaritas. Andrea looked at me and I fell into her black eyes.

"What are you doing over there? Those people don't want us. They think we're trash. You should come back to your hometown. The country's changing. We could do things. We could bring justice to our people. Why do you have to go back?"

In that moment, I had about a million coherent responses. In almost every case, I told her she was right. But for some reason I didn't say any of them aloud. I simply held her face and gave her a long, moist kiss. She returned it, and gave me another. I felt like I was in paradise again. Then she pushed me back.

She shook her head sadly. She didn't understand me. I don't understand myself either. She turned and walked off down the street. It was the last time I saw her. Years later, I heard she was at Tlatelolco in '68 when the army shot at student demonstrators. She vanished that night; I never found out what happened to her or her body. That's why, on nights when I'm a little drunk and get choked up, I imagine she managed to flee from the massacre and take refuge in Guatemala. Maybe she finished her studies and had a daughter who would become a masked hero fighting for justice in our country, just like she'd dreamed.

But I know that can't be true, because in Mexico, films always have happy endings.

PART II

Dead Men Walking

BANG!

BY JUAN HERNÁNDEZ LUNA

Roma

I'm standing in front of the dark barrel of a gun, which is held by a guy who is watching me very carefully and gesturing unsympathetically. I try to move but the guy makes a sign indicating not to or he'll have to shoot. I obey without taking my eyes from the barrel.

I'm on the edge of the roof. Down on the street, there's a parked car with its motor running and lights on. I can't tell if anybody's in the car. I stay quiet, waiting for the guy to tell me what to do. My hands aren't raised, and that worries me, though not too much, because I know that hands in the air don't correspond to the usual script when there's a gun involved.

A shot. If the bullet pierces me, I'll have to try to stop the hemorrhaging, to stabilize my blood pressure. The stupid projectile will probably be dirty, which means it will cause an infection. Wounded, on my back on the roof of this building, it will be difficult to protect my nerves from possible damage; it will be impossible for me to excise the injured parts and save the rest.

Arrrggghhh! Mexico City, such a beautiful, dark sky! About to die, I greet you and watch each elusive red cloud as it floats on the south wind.

Dialogue. Right now there should be dialogue. Threatening phrases that indicate who has the power, and although there's a gun aimed at me, every word suggests I'm the one with the ace up his sleeve.

I contemplate that "ace up his sleeve" and immediately regret it. You shouldn't use clichés, even in real life.

The guy is still in front of me. I have no idea how long it's been. I decide to pull another file from my memory and search for the moment that brought us to this point.

Running. I take quick steps through the street, up some stairs. The neighborhood is totally deserted at this hour, the lights dulled. There are children's toys scattered on the patio. As I ascend the stairs, I feel somebody after me. The rattle of my feet is echoed by even heavier steps that keep me alert.

There are shouts. An old woman peeks out her window and sees my sweaty face. I want to try to make a joke, to say something like *booooooooo*, but the noise of the approaching steps forces me to reconsider, and I keep climbing higher.

When we get to the roof, I try to run but there's nowhere else to go. I turn around and find the guy with the gun who tells me to stop, that it's best to end this once and for all.

I suppose it *is* better to end it, but I keep looking at the gun's barrel and then I see him, and I notice his face, which is scarred by smallpox or acne or one of those damn skin diseases. And then my gaze moves from his damaged face back to the gun barrel.

I reconsider. So it is not a cliff, it is not a ravine, it is not a planet of martyrdom; it is emptiness that fills this four- or five-story building.

From the roof, the smoke of a refinery can be seen to the west of the city. At this hour, it's possible to discern guardian angels leaving to go to sleep; the lights of the city center fusing with the glow of the airport; to hear all the noises from the cars mixing with the *tick tock* of the hearts of little boys and girls; there's a mariachi song; coughing and kissing. The moon rises behind the high tower; the west is bloodred, the south only fog, and I'm left to remember poems . . .

Friend of mine, whom I love, do not age . . .

Running. Running as hard as possible, with everything from childhood in tow.

This is a heavy burden. Childhood's too great a burden to carry while fleeing from a gun.

A smile. Women have twisted smiles. Women are not sincere when they laugh. This is a woman I'm sure I know from years ago, when my hands were trees and planets, and I suppose I knew her and slept with her, but I can't be sure because her hair, which has been done up in a beauty shop, depresses me, and I can see that she's insulting me.

Behind her, there's the guy whose face is scarred by acne or smallpox or some other damn skin disease.

I leave the room and the woman follows me. I think she wants to ask me something.

It takes approximately three days for a corpse's skin to decompose. It fills up with toxic gases that cause sores on the outside, then the skin succumbs, cracks, and the gases are freed. If the corpse is exposed to the sun, it takes less than ten days for everything to collapse, for the flesh to rot and the scent to spread among the living. In the end, only the skeleton remains, and perhaps remnants of the liver, the toughest organ in the human body, the one that most resists decomposition. An irony if the death has been brought on by cirrhosis.

I don't have cirrhosis, nor do I have a body. I am matter floating here on this rooftop where I continue to stare at the barrel of a gun that some guy is pointing at me. To the west, there's the vast, dark stain that is Chapultepec Forest, to the south there's the eternal track of my doubts, to the north the shadow of a blonde who's moving away, to the other north another blonde and another goodbye, until I bring my gaze back to the stain on the west, and again I find the barrel of the gun.

A few days ago: *Tell me that you will not leave me*, a voice whispers in my ear, and I hear the whisper as if it were a siren beckoning Ulysses' ship. And Ulysses—me—I stay firm at the rudder, tied with cords, trying to cross the sea without paying attention to her song. The siren approaches, embraces me, tries to take the rudder and direct me toward an island, but I maintain control and the ship continues its course. Suddenly I notice the ship has ceased to be, it's not even a simple plank sailing in the blue of the ocean; the boat is a bed, the sea is a room, and at my side there is a woman who whispers in my ear, and where the horizon should be, a door appears instead, and it's kicked to pieces by a guy who bursts in with a gun in his hand which he aims right at my forehead.

The siren disappears.

There is no sea in this life.

A flight scene must have its limits. It's impossible to just keep running around the world, there must be boundaries so that certain characters can admit exhaustion.

I am the guy who holds the weapon in his right hand. There's a man in front of me looking to escape, but I stop him and tell him that if he makes any strange movements, I'll have to shoot. My finger touches the gun's trigger and then, totally, completely, I absolutely forget the reason for my aggression.

I don't want to shoot anymore. I don't want this gun in my hand.

A bullet traverses three hundred and twenty meters per second, the equivalent of the speed of a lie, the speed of a bloodthirsty and clumsy and cruel love.

A .45 caliber bullet destroys approximately twenty centimeters of my heart's flesh and leaves an exit wound equivalent to three absences, four goodbyes.

If the emptiness is not empty, if there is no ravine or precipice, if it is only the damn distance of four stories down to the ground, is there any possibility of survival?

Movement.

Stop!

There's a blonde who looked up my name and info and asked to meet me here. The signs are clear: this is an affair. And I, who am not at all stupid, had been certain that a blonde could only be bedded every two centuries.

This was my century.

The guy with the gun shows up midcentury.

The blonde disappears as the century comes to an end.

Anachrony.

When fleeing, it's important not to leave behind the people you love.

A dark tunnel. The same way you come into life, the same way you leave.

Can a tomb be considered a dark tunnel?

Is a vagina a dark tunnel?

Is a penis a dark tunnel?

Jean Valjean carrying Mario through the barreling darkness . . .

The Count of Monte Cristo fleeing through the dark . . .

A stethoscope bringing a sign of life is a dark conduit . . .

Big bang, the damn dark barrel, the fucking quarks are all black holes . . .

Blondes are not good companions for adventures.

Guns are better companions for adventures.

Brunettes are not good companions for adventures either.

The day has not been good.

More than seventy years old, the lady paces the apartment and a cat follows; she watches it with distrust. Perhaps the cat is just anxious, it almost always gets this way when it rains, maybe because of that thing about how cats don't like water, but this is a strange cat, it almost never goes outside so it shouldn't be afraid of the rain; in fact, the lady has never seen the cat outside the house. What's the cat's name? The cat has a peculiar name, her husband says it and the cat jumps into his lap, but for a while now she's been forgetting things, because of that damn disease whose name she would say but it's obvious she's also forgotten that, like with so many other things in this world, and she thinks that at this point in her life it may be better to forget things, to loosen the ballast, like a balloon that needs to stay light to withstand—what do they call that?—yes, the last reverses of life. God, if only she knew what a *reverse* meant, a reverse was a stitch she once learned in her youth which she used when sewing and embroidering and all those things that make a woman more of a woman, manual tasks such as ironing and cooking in order to keep a man happy enough so he'll maintain the household; so now what can a reverse in life possibly mean? How it is possible that life has a reverse, and if it has a reverse then it must have a forward, but she has never experienced a forward. Life has only been difficult, as she certainly knows. They came to that room in the neighborhood forty years before, just for a while, but the years piled up and a while became always and they've lived there ever since, and they had children, of course, three of them, two boys and a girl, all stillborn. That's why they didn't want to try a fourth time—why bring the dead into this world when supposedly this is the world of life? No, no chil-

dren, it was imperative to accept the loneliness and the cats
her husband brought to the house, many of which left, tired
of the lack of food and the smell of poverty and grease all over
the place. Only that one cat stayed with them and lived there,
hiding under the furniture, but that night the cat seemed nervous, perhaps because of the rain. She could smell the scent of
humidity, her muscles sensed it would rain that night, she was
positive. The best thing to do would be to close the window
to make sure the armchair in the living room didn't get wet.
She took a step, watched the cat arch its back, and pushed the
curtains to close the shutters—and that's when she saw a man
hurrying up the stairs. That struck her as odd; perhaps it was
somebody on the way to the roof to collect his laundry before
it got wet on the line, but no—in that neighborhood, the men
never went up on the roof, much less to gather laundry. She
knew she was right when she saw another guy go up after the
first one, with the same haste and a pistol in his hand. There
was a scream but she does not remember, doesn't remember
the words, knows that there were words but she can't differen-
tiate between a scream and an insult; if someone says *tree*, she
thinks *mud*; if they say *scissors*, she relates it to a day of rest,
so she'd rather close the window and wait for the rain to end
and for her husband to come home and for the loneliness to
settle and the cat—that animal called *silence* or *therapy*—to
stop meowing so maybe she can hear herself better, to see if
she can recall a better memory . . .

The barrel of a gun is not just a simple hole, it moves in an
undulating way; perhaps the guy who's holding the weapon is
trembling. Just the same, it could be something other than a
pistol, perhaps a knife of some sort, but if it's a knife then it
ought to be shinier; maybe a knife is easier to avoid. I cling to

this possibility, that at least the sharp edge doesn't have the speed of a bullet. Or does it? Has anybody ever measured the speed of a blade? In any case, what's more dangerous, a blade or a bullet? Obviously, it all depends on the placement of the wound. If the knife damages the femoral vein . . . Do blades shine? I look for the sparkle in the dark but there's nothing there, then everything is a penumbra, and there is no knife, only a gun.

Bang!

Here it comes.

I feel it. My body bends and shakes from the impact. Instantly, I feel the fervor of blood running under my shirt. I am an open vein, a dark channel, a tunnel.

And then Jean Valjean arrives in my tunnel carrying Mario.

And the Count of Montecristo smiles at me as stoically as a rock.

And a cascade of blood slips through my hands.

And I'm here staring at the emptiness of this enormous city.

With its towers and streets.

And those little lights.

And I do not fall.

I hold on to the eaves because I have an ace up my sleeve: the blonde's panties in my coat pocket. My great fetish, a souvenir from a glorious night in bed. I also have the words to tell this guy he can go fuck his bitch of a mother, because motherfuckers like me don't die every day, and then there's a pause that lets me hear the *suusssss* of another bullet grazing my chest.

And soon . . .

My life has been both great and fucked.

Bountiful and idiotic.

Wonderful and absurd.

Why not let it be the same way at the end?

Four or five stories.

A beautiful fall.

This fool will not see fear in my face.

He won't see anything.

I am great.

Is there anything more beautiful than flying toward death?

That's what I do.

JUDAS BURNING

BY Eugenio Aguirre

Calle Tacuba

oly Week 1954 was especially bloody. Thursday morning, agents from the judicial police discovered the mutilated bodies of four women in debris left at a construction site near Peñón de los Baños. There were bite marks on their breasts and genitals, which had been carved up with exceptional viciousness. The presumed killer, later identified as Goyo Cárdenas, had not only raped and profaned their corpses, he had used a handsaw to chop off their heads and dismember the arms and legs.

The evening headline, which appeared in the *Universal Gráfico's* crime bulletin, was accompanied by horrific photos which provoked terror among working-class women in the areas surrounding Mexico City, especially the prostitutes who trafficked around Dolores alley and Dos de Abril Street, who tried to intimidate the authorities with obscene threats: "Either they double the number of security guards on these sinful streets or we'll go on strike and our clients will have no choice but to fuck their wives."

"Things are getting tense," said my father, Don Domitilo Chimal, with dismay, as soon as he finished reading us the unfortunate news. He threw the newspaper on the kitchen table where we were gathered for an evening meal.

My siblings and I didn't fully understand what he was getting at, nor the full meaning of his words. But our mamacita covered her face with her hands and began to tremble like a puppet with Huntington's disease; she ran and locked herself in her bedroom.

On Good Friday the news was no less bloody. Every year from time immemorial, the Ixtapalapa neighborhood commemorates the Seven Mysteries of the Crucifixion of Jesus with a festival that draws thousands of people from places like Azcapotzalco and Xochimilco, so they can experience "live and in person"—as my Grandmother Eufrásica used to say—"the passion of Christ and all the chingaderas those damned Jews did to him." So this festival began like every other, except that the compadritos from the Brotherhood of the Redeemer from over in Milpa Alta, wearing the appropriate attire to represent centurions and Roman soldiers, got drunk early and, with the pretext that Pontius Pilate was "a degenerate puto who was constantly sticking his hand between people's legs," decided to give him a good thrashing, beating him with fists, swords, and spears, which caught the Pharisees, the Mary Magdalenes who accompanied Christ, and the multitude of gentile onlookers on Calvary off guard and made it impossible for them to get away.

"*The Romans are being total jerks*," we heard Tomás Perrín, the newsreader, announce on station XEW, the one our mother used to turn to every night to hear the radionovelas and her favorite program, the *Crazy Monk*. "*They're throwing punches left and right. They already beat Pontius Pilate to a pulp and now—what monsters!—they're striking Barabbas with their wooden swords . . .*"

Later, the newsreader had to yell so that he could be heard over the noise of the firecrackers and the howls of the mob, but he continued narrating how the Romans of Milpa Alta made mincemeat out of Dimas and Gestas, the thieves, and how they tore the cheeks of the poor man playing Christ with the thorns of his own crown, and how this had caused everyone who could to flee and take refuge in the cellar over at Samsom's Cures.

Then the newsreader screamed: *"Oh, they've broken my nose and beat the crap outta me!"* It seemed they'd snatched the microphone from him; all we could hear was chaos—whistles and sirens indicating the presence of the cops who'd arrived to calm the rabble and send the pranksters to jail.

We were all excited by what we'd heard. But my brothers couldn't disguise their disgust at the Romans' transgression. My sisters, contrite and weepy, questioned the heresy and crossed themselves, sure of the punishment waiting for them in the flames of hell. Only our father smiled, with a manic, macabre look, his eyes bright, his brows furrowed, and he announced a decision that had been long in coming and that, to our shame and pain, he would act out the following day.

"It smells of the blessed blood of revenge!" he said with an expression that made my mother shiver. He ignored her, turning to his sons. "Come with me, boys. We still have much work to do."

So, without a word, we followed him to a small shed located in a corner of the yard. There, Don Domitilo Chimal had installed a workshop to make huge dummies, which we called Judases, and which, according to our traditions, are exhibited and burned on the streets of Tacuba every year on Saturday during Holy Week.

The workshop was a mess. There were twigs and reeds all over the place, buckets of glue, old newspapers, pieces of cardboard, scraps of paper, coils, tins filled with brilliant colors of paint, and, leaning against a stone wall to avoid an explosion or devastating fire, firecrackers and rockets in many sizes whose wicks were covered with pieces of foil that came from the gum that the kids in our neighborhood used to chew.

My father had already hung some of the enormous Judases from wires and cords that stretched across the shed, including ones representing Miguel Alemán, president of Mexico, and several of his henchmen, such as Ernesto Uruchurto and the hated police chief, some general named Mondragón that, to the delight of the locals, would be burned the following day. Dad still needed to finish the Judases for Herod; for the execrable Potiphar; for Lucifer, with his horns and trident; and for the popular Samaritana, who, according to local lore, was even more of a whore than Doña María Conesa, the "White Kitten," who'd disrobe in any dive near the Capitol, from the Tívoli to the Catacombs.

We went in and I headed straight to the table where he did the carpentry. Don Domitilo had made the twig frame that corresponded to the Samaritana and which now needed to be covered with newspaper and glue to give it body. But my father shoved me out of the way and, contrary to his usual demeanor, screamed: "Don't touch it, boy! I'm going to do that Judas from head to toe. Help Chema and Jacinto finish the other dummies."

Though his attitude surprised me, I didn't want to argue with him so I immediately got to painting Lucifer's huge body in a rabid red and polishing him with a little rag soaked in turpentine and cola.

We worked all night; by dawn we had finished with the accesories and placed the firecrackers in all the Judases, except the Samaritana, which still needed to have its belly closed, its seams sewn, and a little color added.

"Go and sleep, boys," whispered my father, stuck in his task. "I'll finish this dummy and catch up with you."

I fell asleep as soon as I put my head on the pillow. The only thing I remember dreaming about was a scene from a vampire film I had just had seen at the Chinese Palace and the moans of a woman begging for mercy.

I was awoken by my father's voice ordering me to come with him to bring the Judases downtown. I quickly got dressed and went out where my brothers were lifting the dummies into a covered peddler's cart that we always used to transport them.

We got to Tacuba Street at 10 in the morning. There, Don Domitilo Chimal made the delivery of the Judases to someone at the Central Department who paid him with sticky bills that barely added up to a hundred pesos.

We had started on our way home when my father suggested we get some lunch at the Sidralí on the corner of Madero Avenue and Palm Street, then come back and see the burning of the Judases.

"I want to be sure we did a good job!" he said, with such pride we couldn't have imagined his true intentions.

The lunch was delicious, not just because of the medianoche sandwiches, but because my brother Chema managed to get us some potato pambazos and chorizo in garlic sauce from a vendor outside the Sidralí which we—especially my father— devoured with delight.

"Well, boys," said Don Domitilo at about 1 in the afternoon, "let's go see the burning. They must have hung the Judases by now and I wouldn't want to miss the show for anything in the world."

Tacuba Street was crowded with folks who, entranced with expectation, gazed at the hanging dummies that would be burst on Saturday. Our father elbowed his way through to a place from where we could see, unobstructed, what was going to happen.

The first one they burned was the Judas with President Alemán's smiling face. The rockets attached to the sides of its body exploded with a luminous and cheery sputtering that excited the crowd, which immediately shouted and hurled insults, letting loose the resentments that had accumulated as a result of the abuses against the people during his term.

"Stop acting like a beggar, Alemán, you damn thief!" yelled a worker next to us, and everyone around cheered. "Yes, burn, you presidential thief, so you know what it feels like to be fucked over!"

Then the firecrackers inside exploded, the stomach burst, and the dummy was gutted. The applause was deafening.

One by one, the Judases were burned. The people were overjoyed. Although he seemed a bit taciturn, Don Domitilo couldn't hide the pride he felt when he saw how the dummies he'd made with such care were appreciated. Finally, it was the Samaritana's turn and I noticed my father turning pale. The Judas began to burn on the outside, just like the others, until it was fully singed. Then it exploded into thousands of bits of newspaper and confetti that floated down on the crowd. But this time the paper was drenched in a sticky red substance, with pieces of raw flesh and bone shards mixed in.

The crowd was horrfied. They shook the bloody bits from their heads and shoulders. Some, mostly women and children, screamed as they ran. Only my father, Don Domitilo Chimal, laughed, then spat: "I told you, puta Matilde!" He was screaming at our mother. "I warned you when I found out you were sleeping with my compadre Melitón that a day would come when I'd tear your heart out! Old cabrona, daughter of the rechingada!"

VIOLETA ISN'T HERE ANYMORE

BY MYRIAM LAURINI

Hipódromo

Neighbors Cassette. Side A.
July 16, 2007

[Older people die alone, either from natural causes or because they are killed. The latter happens with such frequency in Mexico City that it is no longer surprising. What does surprise me are these neighbors' voices in unison, as if they can't wait for whoever's talking to finish so they can each tell his or her own story, which made this tape's transcription that much harder. The following are excerpts of what they said.]

Violeta didn't like to talk about her past or her origins. She would insinuate certain things to create different stories. Hers was just one of many stories; there wasn't anything weird about it, nothing particularly moving or vitriolic.

All the neighbors knew her: she was born in that same house. Violeta was part of the neighborhood's Security Commission. As a member of the commission, she was constantly on alert, so that when she saw strangers or odd movements, she'd call the district police. She got along very well with them; in the summer she gave them lemonade, and coffee in the winter.

When you're on the commission, you have to reach out to the district to make sure they'll treat us well. If there was anything scandalous going on in Mexico Park, she'd call the police. If the local representatives allowed music in the park—the kind that rattles your brain—after 10 o'clock at night, she'd call the police.

Violeta watched out for all of us. It wasn't just about the petty thieves or the lowlifes who could impact our lives materially but also the psychological damage that could be brought on by such loud noise in the park.

What does noise from the park have to do with Violeta's death?

It's related to the fact that she had constant contact with the police. They detained Mikel and asked us tons of questions. If she has or had family, it must be distant.

From what I know, her grandmother was very young when they brought her here from a town in Oaxaca during the time of the revolution. She got pregnant by who knows who and had Jovita, and Jovita repeated the cycle and had Violeta; both of them were born in Mexico City. They never went anywhere to see relatives and no relative ever visited them.

They came to live here in 1928. Señorita Micaela already had the grandmother on her staff and the girl, Jovita. The gossips said Violeta was really Micaela's daughter and that's why she inherited the house.

If it's true that she was Micaela's daughter, then perhaps Violeta might have some first cousins, because Micaela had siblings. According to what my mother told me, the family had money, but for whatever reason, they disowned Micaela and left her with just the house and some rental income. It wasn't just any house either, but art deco.

Violeta inherited the house but not the money, so she didn't have any for food or much else. As soon as Micaela died, they cut off the rental income. It was all very dramatic.

But Micaela had paid for Violeta's schooling as if she were part of the family. She went all the way through high school. Later she took embroidery classes, cooking classes.

Nonetheless, Micaela had never stopped reminding Violeta that she was her servants' daughter and granddaughter, and that Violeta had an obligation to take care of her until her last day.

Nobody ever went in that house. I think the last time was when Micaela died, and there were four neighbors there; that wake was pitiful.

We'd see each other on the park benches, at the Security Commission meetings, at the door, and we'd talk then, but Violeta never asked anybody in, not for coffee or soda or anything. Her relationships all existed outside the front door. The only people who went in were those who lived there.

At first, she got by with money from a savings account. Later, she pawned some jewels she'd inherited. When she had no other choice, she began to rent rooms. That's how she made a living. It was always short term, a few months and then *adiós*.

The one who lasted the longest was Mikel; he's been there a year, maybe a little more. Perhaps it's the house itself that scares them off. It's totally dark, no light ever goes in, or air for that matter; it stinks of humidity, of old age—and the smell of old age scares young people. The only one who ever went in and out of the house was Mikel.

⤬

Lalo Cohen came to visit. He demanded that I hold his beloved tape player while he smoked nonstop. He made his demand in that way of his—as if he doesn't have any friends,

even though he is, in fact, a friend in the end. He asked that I
tell him the same story I told the police and the Public Minis-
try. Words upon words, minus some of this, that's what I told
the Public Ministry—because the police had already given
my statement to the PM. Even though it's illegal, I don't plan
to protest, I just want this to be over with.

⌘

Mikel Ortiz Cassette. Side A.
July 17, 2007

I got up at 6 in the morning, like I do every day Monday to
Friday, and on Saturdays when I have to work. Then I do ten
minutes on the treadmill and ten minutes on the stationary
bike. Then I bathe, shave, and dress. With my tie still undone
I made my way to the dining room for breakfast. Pretty much
on automatic pilot, because routines become automatic . . .
or life on automatic pilot creates routines. What do I know?
I didn't smell coffee, or huevos rancheros, or even fresh-
squeezed orange juice. I thought Violeta was still asleep and I
was going to have to make do without breakfast.

When I got to the dining room, the light was off. *Violeta's*
asleep, I said to myself, and cursed. I was in a hurry and it was
dark; it was 6:30 and, though the bank is only four blocks
away, I had to check in by 7 on the dot, otherwise I'd lose my
eligibility for the annual punctuality award.

On my way out, I inadvertently stumbled on a chair and
whatever was on it. I hit it with my knee and cried out. I can't
explain it. In an instant everything rushed to my head like a
crazy hurricane and I somehow knew it was Violeta. I ran to
turn on the light. I saw her and the gasp from hitting my knee

was quickly replaced by screams of horror. She was tied to the chair with a cable. I couldn't bear to look at her and I ran out to the street, scared out of my mind. I paused at the door and my screams turned into a professional mourner's lament. I don't know how much time passed, maybe a minute or two . . . it's just that in situations like that, minutes become an eternity.

That's when Lalo Cohen showed up; he's a neighbor who goes running in the park every morning at the same time. He's like Kant—according to legend, people would set their watches when Kant went out for a walk.

"What's the matter, Mikel?" Lalo asked. I tried to answer. But I couldn't, no matter how hard I tried, choking on my sobs and shaking all over; I couldn't get a single word out.

I started to scream. Lalo plastered his hand over my face. That is, he slapped me so hard my head rattled, and I'm actually grateful because I think it might have been the best way to get rid of my hysteria.

"What's the matter, Mikel?" he repeated harshly.

"She's dead, I mumbled."

"Who's dead?" He was getting angrier and his voice was even more harsh.

"Violeta," I said with a steadiness I didn't really feel.

"Violeta? Are you sure? That can't be. I was talking to her just yesterday afternoon. That can't be."

"I didn't kill her, I didn't kill her, I didn't kill her . . ." I kept repeating, and Lalo squeezed my arm so hard he almost broke it.

"You're being hysterical, she must have just fainted—calm down," Lalo said, and pushed me away from the door. "Come with me and stop screaming."

I decided to follow my neighbor's orders. Hanging on to the walls in the hallway, I went in after him. As we came to the dining room, I covered my eyes with the arm he'd almost broken.

"Fucking A, they killed her!" were Lalo's first words. And the second ones: "We have to call the police!" He went for the phone and I stumbled to the floor, falling right next to Violeta, and lost consciousness.

I don't know if I was awakened by the pain or the *plaf, plaf, plaf* of Lalo's slaps. Whatever it was, it made me leap away from the dead woman and scold my insensitive neighbor: "Why are you hitting me, you beast?"

He acted as if he'd been caressing me. "C'mon, you have to rise to the occasion!"

"To the occasion? I'm going to the bank, I'm already late."

"You're not going anywhere. The police are on their way and you're going to have to give a statement," he said without any sympathy.

I began to shake again and started repeating my refrain: "I didn't kill her, I didn't kill her." I shut my mouth when I saw Lalo raise his heavy hand.

When the authorities showed up, they arrested me as soon as they laid eyes on me, without even asking my name or any questions. But I'm not going to talk about any of that, because you already know all this, I told it all to the commander.

The commander, who said his name was Ponce de León, looked at me with the eyes of a rabid dog until I thought I could see drool in the corners of his mouth.

"Your statement is absolute crap—you haven't said anything remotely useful. Let's try again," the guy growled, looking very secure behind his big desk with his big guns. Sitting like that, anybody can give rabid-dog looks and growl.

"I got up at 6 in the morning, like I said—"

"Fuck that shit! Just answer my questions! You understand?" barked the commander.

"Whatever you say . . ."

"That's right, whatever I say."

An officer came in with some folders and a woman brought a bottle of Coke and left it on the desk next to a pistol.

"This asshole's going to drive me crazy, I can barely keep myself from smashing his brains against the wall," said the one with the rabid look.

"Be cool, commander, don't worry: this fag will give it up sooner or later, he'll give us everything we want."

"Everybody's innocent, even after they've sliced up their sainted mother and used her to make mixiotes," said the woman who'd brought the soda.

"*Here*, everybody's guilty until they prove otherwise," declared the rabid one, and the others offered hearty laughs in response.

The dog finally calmed down a little in the other cops' presence and drank some soda. But nobody calmed *me* down. My guts rumbled in a way I knew meant I should hurry to the bathroom. I asked for permission to go but was turned down.

"So tell me: full name, place and date of birth, profession, whether you can read and write, parents' names, and how long you've been living in the home of the deceased."

"Mikel Ortiz Goitia. Puebla," blah blah blah . . .

"The names of three reputable citizens who can serve as references. Address and telephone number for each."

"I'm not opening a bank account or applying for a credit card, so I don't need to give you references."

"Cut the crap! Just answer my questions. You're driving me nuts, you fucking faggot!"

"Excuse me, but I want to state for the record that I'm not a homosexual."

"If you keep this up, motherfucker, you'll end up being the biggest seapussy on the boat."

I didn't have the strength to argue that he was trying to lock me up without any evidence whatsoever. And that I was innocent. I didn't kill Violeta, who in just a few hours had lost her name and become simply *the deceased*.

"This is going from bad to worse!" shouted the one with the rabid look, and he hit his fist so hard on the table that the guns, papers, phones, and pencil holder danced, and the Coke bottle almost spilled.

But the commander turned out to be so right. This was all nothing compared to what came later.

Neighbors Cassette. Side B.
July 16, 2007

[Same problem as Side A. Impossible to get these people to talk one at a time.]

I want to know why Lalo didn't give a statement. He's a journalist. The police don't usually like it when journalists snoop.

Wait and see what he says.

I was the first to make a statement.

And what did you say?

I told what little I knew about Violeta.

Did you see a strange man or woman hanging around the block a few days ago, yesterday, today, this afternoon, tonight? Did you hear a struggle, screams, anything out of the ordinary?

This neighborhood has been run over by cops, it isn't what it used to be. With a zillion restaurants, bars, theaters, and all that other trash, it's just packed with outsiders.

So how can you tell if those outsiders are potential killers, petty thieves, or rapists? How can you distinguish a cry for help from a wild scream or some drug addict or drunk losing his mind? This is Mexico Park, one of the prettiest places in the whole city, and they killed her right across the street. Nobody saw anything, nobody heard anything.

I saw Mikel say goodbye to a girl in the park while I was walking my dog. It was after 12. We said hello in passing.

Then Mikel couldn't have killed her because Lalo said the murder occurred between 10:30 and 11. That's certainly a relief. Just imagining we might be living with someone who'd kill an old woman makes my skin crawl. It couldn't have been Mikel. She spoke so well of him, and he of her. Besides, he's a very courteous young man, very responsible.

Poor guy, I hope they treat him okay and set him free. It's not fair to blame an innocent person.

Mikel Ortiz Cassette. Side B.
July 17, 2007

The rabid one asked me what time I got home the night of the crime. I told him, "Late, after 12. I went straight to my room, trying not to wake Violeta up." Then he wanted to know what time I usually get in at night. "Between 8:30 and 9, then I watch a little TV and go to sleep because I get up at 6 in the morning."

"But that night you got in after midnight. Why?"

"I went to Mass at 8 at Coronación parish and afterward I talked for a bit with a young woman I've chatted with a few other times. She invited me to coffee and then we went for a walk in the park. We agreed to meet again next Sunday, at the 1 o'clock Mass."

"Let's see . . . you go to Mass every day?"

"No, just on Sundays and special occasions."

"What was so special that evening? Were you going to ask forgiveness for killing your landlady?"

"I didn't kill her! I went because it was the anniversary of my grandmother's passing."

"Name and surname, phone number, and address for that young woman. Is she a student? Does she work? Where? Who does she live with?"

"Beatriz. Her name is Beatriz, but I didn't get her last name."

"Of course—you didn't get her address either. You have a perfect alibi. You know what time your landlady was killed? Do you know, you fucking faggot, that if you'd gotten home at the same time you do every single night, she'd still be alive? But no, that night you got in late, so late you didn't even run into the killer. What a coincidence! Your orderly schedule out of order that night, a stranger entertaining you for hours on end, then you get home so late you don't even need to call for help."

"I didn't kill her! I didn't kill her! I swear to God and the Holy Virgin Mary!"

"Don't blaspheme, you fucking faggot fuck. And you better confess soon because I'm sick of hearing this shit. Your alibi is pathetic."

"I really need to use the bathroom. Please let me go to the bathroom!"

"Denied. And you better not shit in your pants. I can't stand the smell of shit, it drives me even crazier than you do. I swear I'll slice you up with a razor. Do you understand me?"

Of course I understood him. The effect of that threat was to terrify me; the idea of being sliced into a poblana stew paralyzed my intestines and bladder. I thought of Beatriz, so sweet and good, and felt a certain relief, but it was short-lived because the dog was quickly back in action.

"You went out with a young woman, you don't know her last name, her phone number, or her address. You went out with a young woman and you don't know anything about her. If she even exists, she's obviously your accomplice and you're covering for her. While she entertained the deceased, you wrapped the cable around her neck, pulled her hands behind her back, and tied her legs to the chair. So disgusting! How could you do that to a defenseless old woman? Who has the goods? Because it's clear that you killed her in order to rob her. Or did you kill her just for fun? You and that Beatriz are a couple of shits. You're heading straight for a life sentence, you're going to rot in jail."

A life sentence for a crime I didn't commit loosened my bladder and I peed myself. It's impossible to repeat all the insults and threats that rabid man directed at me. All I could think about was saving Beatriz, an innocent young woman who, because she'd had a cup of coffee and a pineapple juice with me, was going to rot in jail. The dog called I don't know who on the phone and there was an instant knock on the door. A guy with a big sketchpad and a bunch of pencils and erasers came in.

"Give me a physical description of your accomplice, buddy, understand? If you lie to me, I'll cut your balls off with this blade or maybe I'll just blow them off."

"Beatriz is . . . tall, slender, fragile, white-skinned. Light brown hair, short. Small eyes, like almonds. Small mouth, thin lips. Her face is longish. Straight, medium nose."

I said the same thing twenty times. The good part was that the dog left me alone for a while. The sketch artist would show me the face and ask questions, then draw in the features, erase a little, sketch again. In the end, Beatriz came out quite beautiful and the dog soon started up again.

"When and where did you agree to meet your accomplice?"

"She's not my accomplice and we didn't agree on anything."

"Okay, smart guy, you didn't agree on anything—but five minutes ago you said you'd agreed to meet next Sunday at the 1 o'clock Mass at Coronación parish. You're not going to get a chance to go to jail—I'm going to kill you first, you piece of shit!"

He jumped from his chair, grabbed his gun, and stuck its barrel in my mouth. He screamed, as if possessed by all the demons in hell: "I'm going to kill you, faggot, I'm going to kill you, you fucking fag, I'm going to kill you, motherfucker!"

My intestines couldn't hold any longer. I shit my pants. There were more screams, more threats, until he finally got tired and called in the others to take me to the bathroom and give me clean clothes and make sure I didn't come back stinking of shit. "That smell drives me nuts," he said, his mouth foaming.

A cold-water shower with Zote soap brought me back to life, rid me of that stink and even some of the humiliation. Back with the hydrophobic, and now more sure of myself, I was the first to speak.

"If you want to kill me, kill me. I don't intend to say another word until you notify my parents and my lawyer gets here."

"It's obvious this faggot spends his days watching gringo cop movies. Let's see, bring me the penal code and I'll read him his rights."

He pulled an issue of *Proceso* magazine out of his desk and made like he was reading it: *"You have the right to remain silent, anything you say may be used against you in court . . ."* As had now become predictable, those around him laughed heartily. None of it did me any good.

Ponce & Cohen Cassette. Side A.
July 19, 2007

[*I've known Ponce de León since I began covering the police beat, what we call* la nota roja. *We were both novices: he'd just finished up at the Instituto Nacional de Ciencias Penales and I at the School of Mass Communication. There's been a lot of water under the bridge since then. He's a man who's close to the law, opposed to torture, and in favor of a professional police force. He likes investigations, technical stuff, analyzing hair and other clues. In other words, his thing is being a sleuth so he can solve crimes. Nonetheless, at no point do I forget my grandfather Levi's words: "Fidarsi é bene, ma no fidarsi é meglio." To that I add my own professional skepticism, and that's why the tape recorder has become a permanent part of my person, like a prosthetic I can't take off, and so I hide it or show it depending on the circumstances. We met at El Chisme, where you can still talk without the background music forcing you to scream.*]

"Mikel Ortiz is driving me crazy. I don't know if he's a psychopath, a total cynic, a con man, or if he just has some terrible problem with his nerves."

"Ponce, have you lost your mind? Mikel is just a naïve boy from the provinces. A practicing Catholic, serious and responsible both at work and in his private life."

"Christians are the worst. They hide behind the church. And that fag unsettles me. I'll tell you something and then you can say what you think. I asked him for some information on the friend who he was allegedly hanging out with on the night of the crime. Initially he only knew her first name, but then he finally gave up her last name and a physical description. With the sketch, we went to the parish where he says he met her. The priests said they'd never seen her before—that is, assuming they're not also accomplices. Although they did give us a clue. On Michoacán Street, we found the Viterbo family. According to the fag, the chick's name is Beatriz Viterbo."

"Beatriz Viterbo? I knew he had a friend, maybe a girl-friend, named Beatriz, but certainly not Viterbo."

"Yes, my friend, Viterbo. We went to the house and were greeted by a skinny old woman who looked just like the Beatriz in the sketch, but about seventy years older. The lady said she didn't recognize the girl in the sketch, same as the priests, said she'd never seen her before in her life. But the best was yet to come. We asked her if she knew Beatriz Viterbo. She said of course, that was her aunt who'd died in February 1929, and she remembered her birthday was April 30 and that for years her family would get together on April 30 to celebrate the woman's birthday. How's that, huh?"

"You're messing with me. Do you know who Beatriz Viterbo is?"

"Of course I know: she's the skinny old woman's aunt who died in 1929 and—"

[Ponce had a little laughing attack and choked on his tequila. He raised his hands. Red-faced, gagging, he coughed a few times and then kept laughing. This went on for quite awhile. In the meantime, I finished both my tequila and his.]

"She's the protagonist in 'The Aleph,' the only Borges story I've ever read—on your recommendation. But I didn't just read it once: I've read it so many times, I know it by heart. And I'll tell you, that faggot was really pissing me off. After I pressed her further, the old woman finally let us in. Proud of what she'd told us about her aunt, she showed us photos of Beatriz. There were several in the living room. Take note of this, because it's crucial: there's a hustler from Xochimilco who is, coincidentally, named Bety. Chema Molina and I exchanged crazy glances, we couldn't believe it—last year I'd made him read 'The Aleph.' The old woman misinterpreted our glances and explained that her aunt had been the most beautiful woman in the city, that she'd had a dozen admirers who were loyal to her even after her death, including one in particular who always came by for tea on her birthday. That's life—she died young, she didn't even have time to get spoiled. I tell you, my friend, I thought I was imagining this. I've seen a lot of bizarre things in my time, but this was the topper. I couldn't believe it."

"I can't believe it either. When did Borges come to Mexico? Did Alfonso Reyes talk to him about her? Did he have other Mexican friends? Did he write 'The Aleph' before he came to Mexico and met Reyes? Or did he meet Reyes when he was the ambassador to Argentina? You didn't ask this woman if she had a basement off the dining room, did you? If not, you're going to have to find out."

"You're going to have to find out yourself, my little friend, you're the literature guy. I have to solve the murder. The prosecutor is squeezing my balls. He wants results, he wants that killer *yesterday*. He hates a civilized society. I'm not even going to tell him this story because he'll send me straight to the last ring in the seventh circle of hell."

"Couldn't it be that the old woman has also read 'The Aleph' and knows it by heart and has set up the whole thing, pure fantasy, out of boredom, or because she's demented, or for some other insane reason?"

"She didn't make it up, there's no fantasy here. Beatriz Viterbo is buried in the Dolores crypt, in a white marble tomb with sculpted flowers and all the decor you'd expect from that time. There's a photo on the front in a bronze oval frame, same as the one in the living room. There are big angels on both sides and the gravestone gives the date of her death: February 28, 1929. The elderly niece, who's the current owner of their house, is Estela Viterbo, and don't even think about identity theft. This woman has a birth certificate, a voter registration card, receipts for her mortgage, and the water and phone bills, all in her name."

"Fuck, what a story! Her name is Estela . . . and the guy goes by on the aunt's birthdays . . . You have to find out more! This can't all be coincidence."

"I'm going to order another tequila to toast all the things you have to investigate. When we were looking at the photos, the old woman couldn't stop talking about her aunt, and then a young woman came in, about twenty-four years old. She said hello, kissed the old woman on the cheek, and left. She was the exact opposite of the sketch: tall, thin, fragile, but dark-skinned, dark-haired, black eyes, large mouth and fleshy lips, a round face, flat nose. No sooner had the door closed than the old woman explained that this was Beatriz, her housekeeper's daughter. I should have done something, ran after her and brought her back, asked her about Mikel Ortiz—but I swear to you I could barely move, I was hypnotized, and so was Chema Molina."

"Shit, shit, double shit! The housekeeper's daughter—same as Violeta, a servant's daughter. That's Mikel's friend Beatriz—he was trying to protect her. He was afraid the same thing that happened to him could happen to her. He told me how you messed with his head, how you stuck your gun in his mouth."

"Don't be ridiculous. I didn't touch a hair on his head, and that faggot can't take much anyway—he's already gone crying to you about it. The gun wasn't loaded, it was just part of the scenery; you think I'd leave a loaded gun within reach of a prisoner? He lied to you. I only pointed it at him, an un-loaded Colt. He probably told you that to explain why he shit in his pants. If I didn't squeeze these guys a little, I'd never get anything. They're all innocent, right? I still have a lot of doubt about that Mikel."

"Well, you can get over it. There's a witness who saw him say good night to the girl in the park, after midnight. He and the witness greeted each other. Besides, the neighbors say he had a very good relationship with Violeta."

"So? What does that mean? They could be accomplices. He described the girl in reverse and instead of giving her last name, he gave her employer's. As far as we know, he—or the murderer—gets to know old women, charms them, treats them well, and wins their trust so he can get inside their homes."

"Ponce, you've forgotten all about being an investiga-tor, about science, even after making such a big deal about it. There are such things as fingerprints, hair, nails, DNA. What's under Violeta and Mikel's nails?"

"There's nothing under their nails. We found fingerprints from the last century and a few more recent ones. The ones on the deceased—on the leather jacket she had on, on her shoes, on the cable—don't correspond with the prisoner's."

"Then why such a speedy conviction?"

"C'mon, don't fuck with me. I'm just holding him. I'm

over my seventy-two hours, but the family lawyer showed up and I was able to negotiate one more day. If I don't get some kind of evidence by tomorrow, I'll let him go. At 8:30 tomorrow, I have to go to the old woman's house to see what I can get out of this so-called Beatriz. When I called to make the appointment, I tried to tell her a little story, that the prosecutor wanted us to talk to her about safety precautions for seniors. She didn't really react at first, and then her response caught me off guard. She said she wasn't in the least bit scared of the Old Lady Killer, that no Old Lady Killer could frighten her. She said she keeps a .22 nearby at all times, that she had it in a pocket in her skirt right then, and that she has excellent aim. Maybe it's the old woman who's your faggot friend's accomplice."

"Fuck you. You're just making stuff up—and stop insulting Mikel. The insults aren't going to clean your conscience. You have an innocent man in jail, and the worst part is that you've known it since the very beginning."

"Excuse me, buddy, he's a fag and a half, and that's that."

"Ponce, you always do the same thing when you screw up . . . it's like your blood gets thin and you stop thinking."

"My bleeding is only because of what I call the *eternal return*. The eternal return is my belief that killers will go back to the scene of the crime. Even if it's not true in 99 percent of the cases, the home of the deceased should *always* be watched. I proposed it in this case. 'We don't have the resources available' was all I got."

"Listen, with all that Borgian stuff I almost forgot to point out that Violeta was part of the neighborhood's Security Commission. She got along well with the guys from the district: lemonade in the summer, coffee in the winter. If neighborhood gossip means anything to you, it is widely rumored that

Violeta was Micaela's daughter and that's why she was her heir, and it's possible Micaela had nieces and nephews circling Violeta like vultures."

"What a mess! All we need now is a blind guy, like in the telenovelas. If Micaela had nieces and nephews, we'll investigate. I'll check in with the district. Lemonade in the summer, coffee in the winter, but those sons of bitches couldn't figure out something was wrong, they couldn't save their friend. This is so annoying. Chema Molina should be here any minute, we said quarter past 8, and we're just a few blocks away. We'll figure it out, one way or another."

"Can I go with you? It would be really helpful for my next article."

"No way, Lalito. And you should be careful about what you write. You might scare off the perpetrator. I don't want the prosecutor, or any of his colleagues, to squeeze me any harder."

"My sources are more sacred than the Virgin of Guadalupe. We're friends, aren't we? I'll wait for you at that bar, El Centenario, in a couple of hours."

"That bar, my dear Cohen, is no longer a bar, it's full of junior assholes who get plastered by their second drink and then scream like a bunch of menopausal bitches. I'll see you tomorrow at 10 p.m., at Sep's, where we can still eat and drink like God intended."

Mikel & Cohen Cassette. Side A.
July 20, 2007

"I'm calling to say goodbye and thank you for your support. I'm returning to Puebla to live with my parents. The cops let me go, but with conditions. They've ruined my life, Lalo. I'm suspended without pay at the bank, though they say it's only temporary."

"I'm sorry, Mikel, that's really shitty. This will be taken care of soon, you'll get your job back and everything will be like it was before."

"They've ruined my life. They've branded me, and those scars can't be erased. It doesn't matter that I'm innocent. I'll be suspected of killing an old woman until I die. I called Beatriz to say goodbye and her sadness froze my blood. The police went to her house. Twice. She didn't tell me much, but I'm guessing it was that demented torturer, Ponce de León. Imagine how they must be suffering. I know that family, and they're really good people."

"Don't be so dramatic. When they find the person who did it, it'll all be forgotten."

"Ha! Careful what you say. Whether they find him or not, my life is still ruined. They took mug shots, front and profile. I was fingerprinted I don't know how many times; I still can't get the ink off. I won't get my job back and I won't be able to get work at any other bank, because I'll be flagged all over the country and possibly even abroad. I don't blame them either, because they have to protect their businesses—how can they have an executive who was accused of murder? There isn't a client in the world who would trust an executive accused of murder. I've also lost Beatriz, who was a good friend and might have become my girlfriend. They've ruined my life. They branded me with an iron, like they do to horses and cattle. They humiliated me, they destroyed me both emotionally and physically . . ."

"Mikel, you'll see that time takes care of these things. Life goes on. Stop crying and get on with your life."

"Lalo, go to motherfucking hell—"

Click.

[Mikel hung up. He was just a kid, still wet behind the ears. He hung up before I had a chance to respond to his curses. There was a black and furious storm in my head.]

Ponce & Cohen Cassette. Side B.
July 20, 2007

[At 10 o'clock I sat down at a table next to a window from which I could also see the entrance. Ponce liked to control windows and doors, entrances and exits. He arrived at 10:05. As soon as he sat down, he sliced a piece of bread, smeared it with abundant paté, and put the whole thing in his mouth. Then he ordered beers.]

"Fuck! I'm really worried that Violeta's murder is going to be just another statistic, another one of those 97 percent unsolved."

"What little confidence you have in your city's police force! Chema Molina talked to the guys from the district who were on patrol that day. At 9:15 they went by the deceased's home. She was at the door talking to a nurse and waved at them, nothing out of the ordinary. We think that the 1 percent will pan out in this case."

"What are you talking about?"

"The 1 percent of killers who go back to the scene of the crime. After the interrogation and the poor description of the nurse that the district guys gave, we sent two of our men to watch the park. They saw a nurse in a cheerful conversation with an old woman and her caretaker. To make a long story short, they hung out for a while, then grabbed her and found a Chinese key on her person. They suspected that the nurse was a he, and so they went to rip off the wig, and *surprise!* There was no wig. But then there was resistance. They discovered that all her documentation was fake. They're interrogating her right now and I'm going to bet this is it. There will be justice for the deceased."

"The deceased was named Violeta. She was born, she lived, she died. She was of this world and now she's just an ordinary cadaver. How sad."

"I can't get worked up about every little murder that comes my way, predictable or not. I'd be doped up and in a straitjacket in a psych ward. But enough of this damn mess. I want to tell you what happened the other night at Old Lady Viterbo's house, though I'll warn you right now that I won't tolerate you making fun of me."

"I'm not going to make fun of you. Let's order now since service is so slow, and let's get another round of beer so your throat won't dry up."

"The older woman quite happily invited us in. She forced us to sit down and offered us tea, a snack, soda, whatever we wanted. *We're working, it's all right, thank you.* I asked if there was a basement under the dining room and she said yes and asked how I knew. I hadn't answered yet when a tall, thin guy appeared, older than her, more dead than alive. She introduced us. 'This is my Uncle Carlos, my Aunt Beatriz's first cousin. A great poet. If you like, he can recite a few of his poems.' I can't describe the look that Chema and I exchanged. My spinal cord froze, just like Borges' did when he went down to the basement to see the aleph, and I felt like we'd fallen into some kind of trap."

"Actually, Borges never said anything about his spine freezing . . ."

"Let me finish. We can argue about the details later. *Great,*

I told the old woman, killing time and trying to figure a way out. The old man pulled some wrinkled sheets out of the pocket in his robe pocket and read: '*There is, among your many memories, one that has been irremediably lost / neither the white sun nor the yellow moon / will see you descend to the core.*' 'You're an impostor! Those verses are by Borges, not Carlos Argentino Daneri,' I screamed. 'I recognize them!' The old man jumped back and tried to speak. 'You're wrong, young man, my name is Carlos Andrés Danielli.' I leapt from the couch as if someone had stuck a needle in my ass. 'Identify yourself!' I screamed. The old man was so scared, his eyes popping out as he looked to the old woman for help. 'Your passport,' I demanded. 'Good lord! This man has gone crazy,' said the old woman as she aimed her .22 at me. Chema stood up, unholstered his weapon, pointed it at the old woman's head, and shouted, 'Ma'am, put your gun down!' I started laughing so hard, I nearly fell over. I couldn't stop."

"Motherfucker! You've lost your mind, Ponce. If your bosses find out, you'll get demoted, you'll end up working as a janitor."

"Tell me about it, Cohen. Fear—fear is a terrible thing. It plays dirty, gets in your way, and confuses you if you're not careful. The laughing attack was a response to fear. That's the subconscious at work."

"But that old couple's crazy too. The guy reads verses that aren't his . . . How did you know they were Borges' if you've only ever read 'The Aleph'?"

"Easy—*memories, white sun, yellow moon*—they sounded just like the blind guy. The old woman threw the .22 at Chema's feet and got silly too, she was laughing and crying, she shook her arms, doubled over, she looked like a puppet. When we calmed down a little, she said, 'I haven't had that much fun in a long time. We must have a party, I have a bottle of champagne in the fridge.' Then Chema and the old man started laughing too. We made a toast to life, to the three Beatriz Viterbos, and to many other things."

"I envy you, and it pisses me off that you didn't let me go with you. How did it occur to you that the old man might be named Carlos Argentino, like in the story?"

"Coincidence, accident, who knows? With all that was going down, logic suggested his name was Daneri. But logic doesn't do fiction any justice."

"Got it. So you hung out with the old couple, just having fun . . . ?"

"With them and with Beatriz Viterbo, the one who was the opposite of Borges'. We toasted to the three Beatrizes: the imaginary one, the one buried in the Dolores crypt, and the housekeeper's young daughter, the one with the unknown father."

"The young Beatriz, she's also Viterbo? . . . So Mikel told the truth and the old woman got her confused with the aunt who died in 1929? We must investigate. This is a bit much, it doesn't seem right."

"I already investigated. The old woman gave her last name to the housekeeper's daughter, made her her heir, sent her to school, where she's earning a master's degree, and, to cap her good work, wants to marry her off to a good man, like Mikel, 'that poor innocent,' she said sweetly. You realize she wants to marry her off to your friend, the faggot from Puebla? I tried to object, to explain we hadn't determined who the killer was yet, blah blah blah. Those three stooges defended the faggot better than the best defense attorney in the country."

"Look at that. Despite a few coincidences, look how different the stories of Beatriz and Violeta turned out to be. And that luckless Mikel left thinking Beatriz didn't want anything to do with him, that he was marked for life."

"I told you he was a faggot. Instead of facing the girl and the old woman and explaining what had happened, he ran away to his mother. He's a coward, that guy."

"Ponce, it'd be better if you just shut up, because you had a lot to do with his running away. Although I confess that right now I could give three shits about that crazy guy. All this smells rotten to me—the three Viterbos, your sudden fearlessness, acting like nothing happened and drinking to madness. Didn't you think for even an instant that they could have drugged your champagne?"

"Well, then I would have gone down to the basement and seen the aleph. What more can you ask from life?"

[*With my head floating from the beer, the tequila, and the interminable literary chat with Ponce, I walked home. As I crossed Mexico Park, I thought of Violeta. I'd met with Ponce to write an article about her, but another story—this one written 1,500 kilometers away—had distracted us from the impact of her death. I remembered that the evening Violeta was killed, she and I had talked for a bit—if exchanging twenty, thirty, forty words can be called that. She had smiled tenderly. I didn't know anything about Violeta, only that she was nice and asked about people's health and their work. In ten years as her neighbor, I never once asked her if she needed anything. Nobody else did either. They erased the smile off that lonely woman's face and killed her for no reason. No one claimed her body, and she won't have a gravestone to remind us she was born, lived, and died. Pretty soon, those few of us who did know her will forget her as well.*]

OUTSIDE THE DOOR

BY ÓSCAR DE LA BORBOLLA

Barrio Unknown

The screams for help crashed through the second-story window with the broken glass. Everybody from the building across the street claimed to have seen the shards hurled like bloody projectiles. The window had turned into a woman's cry, into the sounds of a torn brassiere and broken matrix. She's being raped, some of us thought—killed, imagined others—and we all rushed up the stairs. The metal apartment door was jammed. There was no way to open it; the strongest among us slammed against it unsuccessfully. The next-door neighbor called the police but the line was continuously busy. Let's go get a patrol car, somebody proposed, and two of the other neighbors dashed down to the street. I stayed behind, striking the flat metal of the door with my palms. There was no response from inside and we wouldn't hear anything again. I was soon informed that the condo was vacant and that the owner had put bars on the bathroom windows.

After a while, the neighbors who had gone in search of a patrol car returned with a promise from a couple of officers to come right away; we elicited the same hope from the phone when a bureaucratic voice finally responded and asked us to spell out the address and summarize the facts. Yes, said the neighbor, it happened about an hour ago, around 2 p.m.

But another hour went by and still the authorities didn't

show. We called again; we even tried the Red Cross, the Green Cross, the fire department—but the phones were dead, busy, or rang endlessly without an answer. It was horrible not being able to do anything, feeling so impotent next to that door blocking our way; we were sure the woman who'd screamed was still alive. We couldn't hear a thing but we desperately wanted to help her. Plus, the rapist, the killer, was still in there, because no one had left the place after the screams.

I ran down to the street to look for another patrol car, but there wasn't a single cop, nor an ambulance—nobody. I walked around for a long time and finally, exhausted, I returned to the building, hoping somebody had shown up. But when I saw the others taking action, now with tools, trying to break the locks, I began to curse the irresponsibility of the cops. After all, it was almost 6 p.m. and growing dark and still no help had arrived.

We tried everything with the tools we had: a chisel to loosen the frame, a pickax for leverage to pop the door. But we only managed to chip the point of the chisel and the wall showed barely a scratch. It was even worse with the pickax, because it slipped and cut the leg of the guy from apartment 7, who, accompanied by his wife and a few other neighbors, had to be taken to the hospital, he was bleeding so much.

Then it was after 9 p.m. and nobody had eaten. A neighbor brought coffee for everyone and glorious tacos filled with refried beans. My husband had to stay in bed, she said, because at his age and with all the commotion he's not feeling well. He's put up with a lot, we all said, and we thanked her for the tacos. Go take care of him, someone suggested. Don't worry about us, we understand.

By 11 p.m., those of us who were still there sat down on the stairs, at the foot of that damn door that refused to yield to our demands; worn out, we didn't even have the energy to bitch about the police.

It was useless to continue keeping watch: we couldn't go in and we couldn't hear anything. Perhaps there wasn't anybody alive to help anymore, perhaps it was too late. Perhaps the killer, the rapist, had gotten away before we'd arrived. We weren't sure about anything anymore: our certainties had gradually given way to fatigue. What do we do? asked the tenant from apartment 10; he had to go to work in just a few hours. And me, I have a trigonometry test first thing in the morning, said the guy living in apartment 8. The question of what to do floated about on the stairs for a few minutes until I articulated it again: so what do we do? Somebody proposed we take turns on guard duty until dawn, when we could send somebody down to the station to file a complaint and demand that the cops come. But that idea didn't go anywhere because nobody wanted to stay alone by the door, which could open at any moment and release the rapist or killer; and who could guarantee that it would be just one and not two, and that they wouldn't be armed? I don't live in this building, but across the street, I said. Anyway, I need to go home to see if I got a call because I'm expecting a confirmation on a business trip. We each began explaining our needs and by 2 a.m., without having decided who'd go to the station to file the complaint, we decided to just leave.

The message I was hoping for was waiting on my answering machine: the reservation code for a flight that would free me from Mexico City for a week. I hardly had time to pack my suitcase, call for a taxi, and sleep a couple of hours. As soon as I got to the airport I decided to forget about the screams, to concentrate; I had to get my head straight to deal with my business in Guadalajara, to not mess it up. With distance, talk about work, calls to the office, and the detailed report I had to submit upon my return, there was no way I could think about anything else, and the scene on the stairs began to seem to me more like a nightmare than a lived experience.

A month after I got back to Mexico City, I was crossing the street and ran into the man whose leg had been hurt with the pickax. He didn't know anything either, because his leg had become infected and, between medical appointments and his work, he hadn't had time to ask about the outcome of that ill-fated night, and neither had his wife. After the accident, she didn't want to hear any more about it.

Time passed with the rhythm of daily life, and one night, by chance, I bumped into the guy from apartment 10 at the local supermarket; it was the man with whom I had complained the most about the police for hours in front of that damn door. No, as far as I know, nothing's happened, he said. What? I exclaimed, indignant; seeing him had revived the memory of the screams that came from that poor dead woman, because she had definitely been killed. Yes, he responded, I think they killed her too. But then, I asked, how is it possible that nobody went to the station and filed a report; wasn't the door finally busted down? No, not that I know of, he said, shrugging his shoulders, then added: we all remember the incident, we even lower our voices when we pass the metal door. Even the next door neighbor, remember? The one who called and called the police? She's going to move or maybe she already has; she told me last week when I saw her taking boxes up to her apartment. We must do something! I insisted, furious, as if I were determined to go and personally file the report. But you, why would you commit yourself to going to the station? You don't even live in the building. I stared at him; it had been almost two months . . . The supermarket cashier then said: That will be 275 pesos. Do you have a parking ticket for validation? I handed over the money, mechanically, picked up my change, and said goodbye to the neighbor.

PART III

SUFFOCATION CITY

A SQUIRREL WITHOUT A TREE

BY ROLO DIEZ

Centro Histórico

I was still very young and had barely experienced heart-break when I first saw the bird with enormous wings. The wings were so great they covered the sun and threw shadows over an entire Arab city, across those churches with multicolored towers, round and pointy like a spinning top. I saw the bird in Graciela's storybook. I see it again now, when there's nothing left in the city, only the beating of the wings and me; it's colder here than in Reclusorio Sur prison or Nevado de Toluca.

Black coffee, a roll, and a pastry—I've always had the same breakfast. Although sometimes a beer is the one and only remedy for mornings when the sun is blinding and a man regrets that last pint. But now I need my coffee, my roll, and my pastry. Maybe because it's 3 in the morning and the last time I had a bite to eat was yesterday afternoon, or because of that cold strip between my back and my guts, or because there are only two of us on this empty street and two is a terrible number at this hour, with everything I still have to do, and do without any help or witnesses.

Let me tell you, at this hour, on these streets, it's best if you're from the neighborhood. Around here, God helps who-ever helps himself, everybody knows what's going on, and no one expects the head of government to actually solve any problems or for the best fighter to win in the ring. Friendly folk do not abound. Respectable people walk determined to just get home in one piece and with a few bills still on their bodies. The strong survive, that's the law of the land.

There's another guy on the street and he moves as if he were alone, as if it were 10 in the morning and the Squirrel didn't exist; he ignores me and that must mean he wants to control me. I tuck my right hand into my jacket, cover the handle of the sevillana, and squeeze hard to feel it. I took this knife off an aimless gringo leaving the Bar León, up to his ears in local bourbon and without a clue where his hotel was. A gift. He'd even lost his shoes. I decided to go easy and just take the knife. A useful beauty, the best thing in the world.

The guy keeps going. It's three blocks to my house and then the street is mine. The cold air on my chest shakes me to the core. It's a good time to go into La Cotorra and ask for an aged tequila and a hot snack. But it's closed. No way. It's late.

I think about the One & Only. Graciela is the first woman with whom I've resorted to begging, and she'll be the last. Like Jose Alfredo drunk on love, like an encyclopedia of boleros. I've shown more appreciation for her than for a box of gold Rolexes, a new car, or a whole year in Acapulco. Has anyone ever seen me behave like this with any other woman? Not a one. Our names must be written in the Book of Destiny. Celebration and quarrel always come in the wake of the bird in Graciela's book.

Centuries ago, the One & Only was just a flower of promise and great wings grew from my back.

We lived deep in the neighborhood, my Tía Clodomira and me, in the Republic of Guatemala between Rodriguez Puebla and Vicarious Leona. She took me in after I was abandoned by my mother's misfortune. She called me Squirrel out of love, and I knew that in her skirts I'd find the first and most exclusive hideout in which to seek refuge. Clodomira worked in a clothing store and she'd leave me playing on the patio. "Do not move from here, Squirrel." "No, Tía." "Wait for me." "Yes, Tía." Pretty soon I learned to go from patio to patio, and from the patios to the street. Scared to death, I began to wander and made my way around the block. Haven't stopped since. I must have been about four years old then and that's my earliest memory. Before then, I can't picture anything. Although sometimes, on nights when the world crashes in on me, I believe I've glimpsed cloudy shapes and shouts that surround and beat me with an incomprehensible ferocity. Frightening things, which I neither recognize nor understand, but which haunt me, force me to turn on the light and smoke one cigarette after another until I see the sun come through my window.

I think about the One & Only and I know that girl— whom I first met when she was just a gaudy, awkward caterpillar, and whom I later witnessed as a butterfly—was whom I truly loved. I say it now because I don't know if I'll ever say it again. I remember when I first went to the circus, my aunt's fiancé—a stocky guy named Reynaldo who was a coyote in Monte de Piedad—told me to keep my eye on the trapeze artist because he might fall and kill himself and it would never happen again, even if I showed up with a fistful of bills and paid a hundred times the ticket price. "Good things only come around once," said Reynaldo, "and if we aren't ready to dive in, we risk being left out, forever regretting." It's not that Reynaldo was a wise person, because if he were wise he wouldn't be in prison, but for anybody who depends on hustling to eat, his words make sense.

* * *

At fifteen, I was making plans and holding on, barely passing my way through high school, looking to learn more and trying to keep up with Graciela from afar. We weren't friends anymore. The One & Only despised our little gang from Guatemala, our tricks to get money, the zits that tormented me, and even my skill at beheading rats with a slingshot.

In the gang, it wasn't a good idea to let on that you were in love; in fact, it was disastrous, because the guys had a cruel laugh reserved for anyone who developed soft feelings more appropriate to old women and fags. Like the men in bars from olden times, the gang didn't tolerate anybody in uniform, or women. An honorable "Guatemalteco" only concerned himself with those sweet enemies when it came time to steal their panties and their hearts.

Actually, keeping the secret wasn't that hard in the gang. It was all about taking on an attitude appropriate to a Guatemala hustler. "That chava belongs to me, one way or another. Nobody better touch her cuz she's mine." Still, it's hard to love somebody who looks at you like you've got eight legs and can crawl up a wall. But it wasn't always that way. A lot of time passed from the moment that little girl came to the back patio with her book in hand, to the day the nymph stopped coming, to the time that woman refused to even greet me. There were afternoons when I took to reciting romantic songs and taking her picture when I saw her lower her guard for a moment, revealing a gentle moistness about her eyes and a bloom in her cheeks. An anxious and flattered woman is an open window to anyone who knows how to look into it. I swear I felt like Juan Diego greeting the Virgin of Guadalupe. But each and every time, just when a feeling seemed to be stirring inside the One & Only, just like a chick pecks away at its shell in order to come to life, something would happen, and Graciela would again notice the marks on my skin, and she would wrinkle her nose as if something were rotting and then everything got fucked up again. Furious and desperate, the only thing I could think to do was insult her, bring her down with savage commentary to erase her sense of superiority, twist her rejection of me into fear of the streets. Later, when she was fifteen and I was eighteen, love and scorn were the same thing.

At the plazas in Loreto and La Soledad, I had money to ease things and met adventurers who didn't faint over smallpox scars. Some became my friends. We ate sweet rolls, drank muscatel, and sometimes waited out the night to see the sun rise. The moment is so magical there in the center of the city that you're willing to see Aztecs emerge from the ruins; you're willing to believe the most fantastic legends. "Fuck her good and she'll be yours forever. You don't have any other option. Easy or hard, if you're the first, you have a chance. What's to lose? Don't be such a lightweight; women like men who are determined." They didn't know Graciela; they were talking about other women.

I pursued Graciela and she rejected me. Like a dog begging for a caress I went after her. I pleaded with her a thousand times in a thousand ways, I robbed a car to take her for a drive, I pressured, I threatened, and, in the end, I hurt her so badly that a hundred years of regret won't be enough.

If something has to happen, it will. The black hour came when a passing helicopter reminded me of that bird, when my unfulfilled dreams disappeared in its flight, and then there was a knock on the door to the patio and there she was—fruit for the taking in a flowered dress—precisely on a Friday when

Clodomira had warned me that she'd be late. In that fatal second, I knew that we had reached a point of no return. Because . . . could I have done anything differently? . . . What else could I do, I ask, what else could I do? . . . Or must the Squirrel call the garbage man, give him some money, and say, "Just stuff me in your truck and toss me in the incinerator"?

What happened that afternoon was unfortunate. First, because it's unbearable to hurt the woman you love . . . A crazed and empty-headed bato, a head filled only with tequila and anger and marijuana, so that you can't think or regret or get it together to disappoint the prostitutes who hope to see you do it and finally stop acting like a fag . . . obsessed with finding disdain in the face of the beloved . . . having made the ridiculous decision to make her pay for not loving you . . . Add it up and none of it makes sense. It was impossible to even hope that the magic of the first time would transform her rejection into love, like what happens in stories and movies we've all seen and know: first, the leading lady throws a furious tantrum; then—nobody knows how this happens—passion emerges.

But passion failed to show this time—Graciela didn't change and that was the first misfortune. Or perhaps, who knows . . . The second came in terrible words: "You are going to pay. You are going to die for this." Her eyes were stone cold when she said this, staring right at me so I'd know she was serious.

Truth be told, nobody gets through life keeping promises. If you don't believe me, just ask the president. Although Graciela is another story. If she says, "It's gonna rain," it's best to take an umbrella. "You are going to die for this," said the One & Only. I fell to my knees; sick with remorse I swore eternal love, I promised to live to take care of her, I begged. But it was like talking to a wall, like pleading with a statue.

After that, I only searched for her once. I did it because I still had some hope left, and before I gave up the fight I needed to know once and for all if the prostitutes were right. I just looked for her one more time. I saw her coming and I stepped in her path. Graciela saw me and erased all my doubts. Erased my doubts and my will to live as well.

If I didn't suffer too much it was only because there wasn't much time. Finding food in this city takes a whole day. Any kind of enterprise requires surveillance and work. Even robbing a gas station means forgetting about Bonnie and Clyde and studying the situation first. Secrets are revealed by going through the details. There might be money at certain times but not at others; the architecture and number of employees will determine how many men are needed to make the assault; depending on the plan, you can pass for a customer or leave in a customer's car; you have to know the police patrols in the area, find the best route for a getaway, anticipate alternate paths of escape . . . myriad problems to solve and the man-hours needed to do it. That way, with days and nights turned into work, pain and love are excessive. In other words, romance and regret have a better chance in the movies; on the streets, you have to break your back.

Pretty soon I was sick of Guatemala. I got myself far away from Graciela and from the scene of the crime. I left the neighborhood, I left the city itself, I traveled the country, coast to coast and up and down. And although the newness was exciting at first, in the end it just seemed like going around the block a million times. New landscapes and different faces hide the fact that, no matter where you are, laws apply to everybody, prison bars all look the same, and cop bullets are cop bullets.

I wandered for four years. Now and then I returned to the city, I visited Clodomira on the sly and found out how things were going in the neighborhood. That's how I learned that Graciela was now with a heavyweight from Morelos. According to the rumors, some dude tied to the Gulf cartel. And since gossip and perversion go hand in hand—they're certainly kin—I also found out the street had me pegged. Guatemala invented what it didn't know. Something had happened between Graciela and the Squirrel, something grave, mysterious, and truculent—everybody's lack of imagination was so depressing that they all thought the same thing: "That cabrón Squirrel must have raped her." The third nugget of info claimed that, to gain points with his lady, the Morelos heavyweight had put a price on my head. I couldn't believe it. In the neighborhood, people talk because the air is free. Anybody with a mouth can join the cotorreo and if they don't have a good story to tell, they just make stuff up. But as the love of my life, Graciela would have never accepted such savagery. I didn't worry then and I'm even less worried now, when the winds seem to have shifted in the neighborhood. This month's news is that the Morelos heavyweight was put on a boat and is resting comfortably in La Palma, the high-security prison. So much for him and the stories concocted in Guatemala. I don't know why I bother with somebody I don't even know. Must be the loneliness, which grows like pestilence at dawn.

"Your thing is melancholia," some guy in La Cotorra dared to say to me once. "You hurt everywhere and you don't know why. Love gone bad, fucked up." I showed him the sevillana and the guy shut up. But tonight, dizzy and confused, trembling, I remember what he said.

* * *

Three-thirty in the morning, three more blocks to my house on this deserted street, and I'm thinking about black coffee, a roll, and a pastry. My aunt goes back and forth from the table to the stove. In the patio there's a little girl playing with a storybook. I like to read to her and make up stories in which the bird with enormous wings flies us all over the world. Graciela and me in the clouds, looking at houses and fields from above. The little girl's a big burden but she'll be pretty when she grows up. The sweet, hot coffee does me good for a moment, but then there's that ice plunging through my chest, the helicopter above me, that room in the neighborhood and the promise made, my list of creditors, and that man who got put away. As soon as I get up off the ground and this cold leaves my back and the taste of blood disappears from my mouth, I'm going to go tell Graciela I'm sorry, that I've always wanted her, for real, like a man, like it must be, but then I fall.

GOD IS FANATICAL, HIJA

BY Eduardo Monteverde

San Fernando

"F ather . . . I accuse myself of having changed my sex."

"Is that so, hija? Me too."

The incense in San Fernando Church veiled the confessional in mist. To the side of the Epistle, an altar boy with the crusty face of a seraph, dressed in a red habit, rocked a small brazier. He was just a kid, with scrawny limbs like those street urchins who surrounded the temple.

"What do you do for a living, hija? I'm entranced by your perfume."

"At night I'm a dancer and by day I search for lost children, though I haven't found any yet."

"You're a crook," said the priest.

"It's not what you think. In fact, I used to work for the state police."

"I used to be a nun. Shall we go outside for a stroll?"

"You're not going to absolve me?"

"I'll take care of that later. Let's save ourselves the confiteor. I'll confess that it's *you* who came to *me*—I consider the admission that you're an ex–police officer a humble act of solidarity."

In another confession booth, incense threaded like steam in a bog around the feet of a different priest wearing torn Nikes; it snaked in under his habit and wafted toward his crotch. It was the breath of Fernando III, medieval king and canonized flagellator, whose weightless sword was displayed at the altar and hovered above his spare crown, above the devout women in their prayer shawls. The warrior wore a metal belt that cut into his flesh despite many layers of mesh. His spirit traveled from the incorrupt body in Seville to watch over his dominion in New Spain.

The penitent and the confessor strolled out together. They walked from the portico to a tainted lawn, careful not to disturb the sickly, glue-addicted children huddled about.

"Check out their stomachs, hija. Those strange cavities are ulcers, and look at that one's sunken skull. Very few of them are worth eating. Not even a cannibal would be tempted."

"What about the man who came over here a few days ago?"

"The guy who ate his lover? He didn't dress his victim very well, according to Próspero, my neighbor in the confessionals, a baldhead who walks around in torn sneakers. Would you like to catch the cannibal?"

"If Madre— Excuse me. I caught one—well, *I* didn't, but I was there when they caught him, Madre— Excuse me again."

"I'm not offended by the gender confusion. We are surgical angels." The priest covered his head a bit more with his hood, allowing only the slightest glimpse of his waxen scalp. "This church is Mexican baroque, which is kind of poignant, don't you think? Scary, isn't it? Look how the sky has turned purplish. It's because of the smog; in a little while it'll turn blue. This city always manages to get drenched in liturgical colors. If you want to find lost kids, go down to the sewers and poke around in the drains with a wire . . . Let's go down to the pantheon."

He shook his brown habit, waving away the stains of urban shame. They were greeted by an immense pink marble funerary urn in the center of a modest garden which contained the petrified remains of a fierce military man, a conservative Indian shot next to Archduke Maximilian of the Mexican Empire. They walked among the graves in the San Fernando pantheon under the city's lecherous gray sky.

"Did you use torture when you were a cop?"

"On men, but it wasn't what you think."

"*Torture*. Don't be afraid of the word. You were no doubt turned on by their erections when you used the cattle prod on them. Electricity is miraculous—like the tolling of San Fernando's testicle."

"Are you still listening to my confession?"

"*I* confess once again that I was waiting for you. You remind me of an old lover. Let's see . . . San Fernando whipped the flesh of his soldiers with barbs. Times are changing; you have to adapt to technology. Did you get aroused?"

"I was a bit soft. My peers harassed me and I had to show I had balls, so yes, yes, I got aroused. I'd caress them after they passed out."

"Who did you sleep with?" asked the priest.

"With Commander Pérez . . ." The girl practically fainted after saying this, her back to the cross, her face like a Mediterranean spring. The city's dense air shrouded her white Gap pants and aquamarine Zara T-shirt—flea market bootlegs—in a gray aura. If she'd been naked, an infantile San Juan de Dios would have covered her breasts with his hair like sea foam, Renaissance style.

The hooded priest took her by the hand. "Look at the grave of Benito Juárez; he gave the order to shoot the soldier buried at the entrance. He was an Indian too. That's Mexico City: Everything's mixed. Fatality and hope are tangled in the same vine. This pantheon still smells of death. Supposedly, *everything* decomposes in the tropics. But some things are still here even if you don't see them. Look at the tombstone that says *Isadora Duncan*—she's here, but she's also buried in Nice. That's how Mexicans are: an admirer had this cenotaph made for her to put next to Juárez the Indian. *This* is miscegenation!" The priest's flowing sleeve stretched as he gestured toward the cemetery. "Tell me about your erections."

The conversation became a murmur reverberating in the crepuscular traffic. When they arrived back at the church, the priest closed the aged oak portico. They made their way down the middle aisle, past the pews now empty of their beatific penitents, whose scents still lingered. A ring of lights like sentries revealed a painting that covered one wall of the nave; hundreds of these sentries guarded a multitude of friars on their knees, gazing up with admiration at the seven martyrs of Ceuta and the seven from Morocco; they praised the Lord on a cross sprouting fir bulbs, and the nine hierarchies of the celestial court in the sky: archangels, thrones, powers, dominions, cherubs, seraphim, angels, principalities, virtues. The painting emanated shadows. A gloom grew on another wall, barely touched by four handfuls of fire coming from the cave of Bethlehem—four is a sacred Indian number. Above the cave, in the stormy sky, a cloud curled up the spiraling stream that represented the native water, water and fire—*atl* and *tlachinolli*—and an irascible San Fernando stood on the altar in a niche surrounded by chiaroscuro coils worked by Indian hands.

Night fell on the children scattered around the church and vestibule. A sad figure in a Burberry raincoat bought at the Galleria on New Bond Street in London turned his back on them. A police officer in Mexico earns enough to take a group vacation, and to finance a sex change for a favorite subordinate. This was Commander Pérez. He looked languidly at the vestibule, raised his eyes to San Fernando, King of Castile, flanked by four angels. For him, a devout Christian, San Fernando was a phantom. The police officer's spirit had taken a different path, one with lyrics to boleros and desire for a young body whose sex he had changed, who now accosted his soul. He breathed with a deep, loving sadness.

Inside, the penitent and the confessor continued through the thick darkness of the hall of tombs. A bell rang for the dead. The altar boy with the small brazier let it toll, sighing when an airplane passed above the church.

"You know what the brains are like in those kids out there?" said the priest. "Like marine sponges with a thousand eyes. They stink of toluene or whatever it is they put in that glue. It perforates their brains. They can be marinated and boiled, then the scent goes away. Do you know what they taste like? Are they the lost ones you're trying to find? Incidentally, you haven't even told me your name."

"Nausícaa," replied the girl.

"How sophisticated. Who gave you that name?"

"Commander Pérez."

"I would have named you Xóchitl Fernanda. It's much more Mexican. My name is Diego Tonatiuh. Before, I was called Temeraria, *reckless*. Blame it on my father, an anarchist from Aragón who took refuge in this mixed-up city; he was mestiza like me. They say I killed him with a dirty look for making me become a nun."

At that moment, the altar boy with the small brazier peeked over the pulpit and asked, "Do you want to stay the night?" He looked like a little cherub frolicking after the gentle figure of the Archangel Michael, whose lance had been stolen to skewer the devil. Neither penitent nor confessor responded.

Finally the girl spoke: "I have to go to work, Father . . . And I never asked you: how long has it been since you changed your sex?"

"Before the deluge, before the plagues of Egypt, before the First Sun, before the Nahui Océlotl that lasted 674 years, and before all those people were devoured by tigers. Then came four more suns, and then the last: San Fernando."

The priest suddenly fell to the ground in ecstasy and Nausícaa thought the altar boy was speaking through him, the nasally voice of a cherub through the throat of an old monk: "*Pange, lingua, gloriosi corporis mysterium, sanguinisque pretiosi* . . . God is fanatical, hija," he said, convulsing. "He makes me say things, see and hear what's not real. The body is a mystery and blood is precious . . ."

The altar boy came down from the pulpit, helped the priest up from the tangle of his robe, and whispered something in his ear. When the priest saw Nausícaa's astonished look, he told her to pay no mind, it was just an apparition in transit. He recovered his poise, his voice turning deep again.

"If I were to say it in Castilian, it would be something like a soul en route to . . . Heaven? Limbo? I can't tell you for sure. Since we're dealing with a street kid, I don't even know if he's been baptized. If I were to say it in Mexican, then it would be a *teyolia* disguised as an altar boy on his way to one of the four worlds of Mictlán, an inferno for elders from these parts, something akin to a *spirit* to us Christians. Where will it go? He's too much of a lazy ass to be leaning on the teat tree in Chichihualco and sucking away for all of eternity. Will you let me see your tits? I don't like to call them *chichis*; it's a Mexicanism that doesn't sound right to me—remember, I have Aragonese blood. Anyway, let's go to the sacristy, we'll be safe there: the soul, *teyolia*, or whatever you want to call it, told me there's a man outside from whom we can only expect the worst."

The altar boy ran off to hide in the chapel's shadows. Nausícaa glanced his way, and the kid laughed uproariously, then quickly disappeared.

Standing before the façade, Commander Pérez raised the collar of his raincoat and exhaled a sigh of longing. He restrained himself from kicking the children in the vestibule and retraced his steps, like always. His bodyguard was there waiting for him next to the squad car and they returned to the police station.

Pérez took the day's bribes, headed down to the dungeons. The cannibal who had been arrested a few days before near San Fernando was there in a moldy cell; a grated night-light dripped stalactites of horror. The scrawny cannibal who had devoured his lover lay trembling there on a concrete bench.

The commander's daydream about the end of the workday, when he would go home to his wife and children and take refuge from his love for Nausícaa, was interrupted when his deputy arrived with the kitchen gloves and baseball bat.

"It smells like human flesh, like heat," said Nausícaa.

"Don't profane this sacristy with your lies. In this city everything filters through, whether it's sewage or fried food, mint, epazote, thyme, marjoram, incense, or myrrh, you know what I mean? I used to wear perfume when I was a nun, after the abortions, because it made me feel less dirty; it was a pirate essence, a scent the gods could breathe. I stopped being an impure sister and became the Black Brigand. You say that it smells like human flesh. Are you suggesting—"

"No, no, Father Diego Tonatiuh. I recognize the smell from the incident with the cannibal. The case was assigned to Commander Pérez, the guy I told you about. I worked on it too. It was the neighbors who called it in. They'd been complaining for more than a year that something smelled weird in a house near where they lived downtown. We went and we found—"

"More details, hija. Carnality is so exciting."

"Commander Pérez kicked down the door and stormed in with a submachine gun. There were about five of us, and the ones behind me kept pushing until they had the barrels of their guns you know where."

"Up your ass."

"That's what they always did to me. They said I was a *puto*. We caught the cannibal stirring a saucepan with a wooden spoon. I don't know exactly what was in it but it smelled like meat. One of my buddies pulled out his ranger knife and carved into a human leg. We were all dressed in black; we wore knitted caps. Somebody opened the fridge and found two women's heads. I got dizzy from the smell of the stew—can I say stew? Commander Pérez shoved the cannibal's head into the pan. One of the other cops pulled me into a room filled with porno magazines and raped me. I let it happen, and then the commander came in and broke the other cop's face. He totally messed him up. There were teeth on the floor."

"Would you eat an altar boy with cous cous à la Mexicana?"

"We caught the cannibal but he impregnated me with that stench. That's why I use so much perfume."

Perfumed bodies, contraband perfume, insect perfume, thought the priest (the ex-sister, the nun of nuncas, Sister

Reckless of the Nuncas). It was too late now for regrets, but she certainly wasn't going to rob a bank again just to finance a sex change. She was getting older and had little desire to be with anyone except that one man, even though they couldn't be together anymore because a monkey wrench had been thrown in their destiny. Father Diego Tonatiuh had had a love, a great love, the only true love of his life, and the police had killed him with their wretched justice—they fried his ass with the prod. He had met his love at the convent of the Franciscan Conceptualists, where he'd practiced curettage as a nun, when the man brought his pretty girlfriend in to have an abortion.

The soul of the priest moved away from Nausícaa. He was lost in his memories, gazing upon a canvas of the Immaculate Conception, a childish virgin standing on a windy platform held up by numerous friars in fine embroidered robes; above them, the shield of San Francisco, five scars and white hairs strewn on a book. The priest recalled himself as Sister Reckless standing in a cloister of orange trees. She was rubbing orange blossoms on the hands of the man who brought the girl to get an abortion. It was love at first sight. The man was struck by the nun's masculine poise. She of the manly presence was, in fact, a small-time bank robber, and he would soon join her in this pursuit. Mockingbirds sang in the halls, canaries twittered, potted azaleas flowered when he whispered in her ear: "Like foam floating on the mighty river, my azalea, life has swept you away in its avalanche." She had taken a book from her habit, pointed to a painting that had been laminated with mold since the conquest: framed by flowery jungle vines, a centauress with adolescent legs and wearing huaraches climbs on a monkey; the monkey caresses the woman's breasts with one hand, masturbates with the other. She told the man that this is how his love should be, a faithful rendition of the colonial impetus painted and imagined by Mexican Indians and Andalusian friars with a good dose of the medieval. She read: "*My spirit pushes me to write about the metamorphosis of bodies into new ones. O gods! Since you have also changed, do not hesitate, inspire my efforts and take this poem from the world's beginnings all the way to our times.*" The sister had then entered the abortion room and provided the patient with a triple dose of sodium pentobarbital. There was staff at the convent to take care of these problems, and not long after this, there was Sister Reckless of the Nuncas stumbling along the Great Canal, dependent on the generosity of the police. That's where his lover wound up.

Father Diego Tonatiuh's mind returned to San Fernando, his breath flew from the cloister of orange trees back to the sacristy and retook the conversation with Nausícaa.

"A few days ago they caught another cannibal close to here, the one we were talking about, the fag." His voice turned nasally again, vibrating under the hood until it seemed almost hysterical. "If you use perfume it's because you're a whore. Don't make it sound like it's because you have the saintly smell of a devout nun or because the smell of flesh bothers you. Oh, please forgive me for the whore comment. I have been contaminated by Mexican machismo. Just give me a moment to get back to my normal state."

"Where are you taking me?" the girl asked when the priest abruptly grabbed her arm. "This stinks of human flesh. I don't want to go. Let me go! I'm not a whore, I'm a virgin!"

"That is the true abstention, the seventh seal, the rest is macho sodomy and it's just not worth it . . . although it has its charms."

As Father Diego Tonatiuh dragged her out of the sacristy, the stench of flesh burrowed deep in Nausícaa's heart and burned itself there. The priest noticed this and told her it was because of Father Próspero, who lived in an apartment in the building next to the parish and liked fusion cuisine—very modern for that priest with the torn sneakers. All the Mexican baroque crashed down on her: Nausícaa lived in that very same building.

The girl shot out of the church, desperately seeking an escape. She stumbled on a glass box and came face-to-face with a Christ overwhelmed by millennia of drops of blood.

"Up his ass, hija! Tickle his balls with that cattle prod!" the priest screamed hysterically. "He's a fanatic and he's accustomed to such passions. You can do whatever you want to him without remorse—he's merely one more prisoner here. Scream at him, humiliate him! Nobody can hear you, not even the police. Ha! You can't even hear yourself!" The priest's voice echoed like metal splinters through the temple.

In that corner of Mexico City, the sun did not set or rise. It was the sky that was lowered or raised. Night fell on Nausícaa with a layer of reddish soot, like the familiar everyday sky from which people took refuge, trapped in their homes. The young woman gazed on the darkened buildings, a light here and there, the beams of a passing car. The steam from the motors that ran all day now rose from the sidewalk, a dam where the street children made their camp inside the vestibule of San Fernando. To the left and right of the Holy King, Domingo and Francisco watched these creatures ignoring the lessons of discipline. They slept sated with glue, others sweated the glue out in collective fornications. Nausícaa remembered her job. They would scold her. She moved toward a pile and looked at the kids engaging in unseemly activities.

"This is the true sexual liberation," whispered a voice in her ear.

Instinctively, she reached for her gun, a useless reflex; she'd been unarmed since she'd changed her sex.

"I am Father Próspero. I have seen you dancing on tables. You're never entirely naked. How did you get that privilege? When you finish your performance, they shout at you and humiliate you—do you like being humiliated?"

A street sweeper crept by.

When Nausícaa heard the word *humiliation*, it struck her like one of those badly pirated DVDs, and the images came to her, one after another, of her debasement at the hands of her fellow officers, the resentment they felt at her middle-class ways. Maybe they would have had more respect if she'd behaved like a whore from Veracruz and let them call her *Negra*. The DVD paused on an image from adolescence, when his father caught him fucking the maid's son. He ran to the woman who'd raised him, but he was sent off to become a cop, to get the *puto* out of him. It didn't work; his peers did whatever they wanted with him until Commander Pérez, his guardian angel, showed up. That night Commander Pérez paced, unable to read *The Odyssey: They had consumed Nausícaa and the slaves. No sooner had they gotten rid of her veils and played, then there was Nausícaa, with her snow-white arms, singing.* His protector, his guardian angel . . .

Her stomach began to turn, or maybe a psalm came to her, and she confessed to Próspero the incident with the servant's son, and how he had massaged the private parts of those who had been tortured. The priest smiled, and her mouth went dry.

"What are you doing here at this hour, Father?" She spoke now in a calm, solemn tone, but there was coldness in her eyes. "Did you come to bring them something to eat?"

"No, I came to eat them."

"Are you a sinner?" Tears bubbled from the heat of Anáhuac's merciless night.

"I'm a goliardo, a clerical nomad," the priest answered. "As they say: *To follow gods and goddesses / will be a good sentence / because networks of love / have already captured adolescence.*"

A squeak filtered through the night. Then there was more noise, more squeaks from the fornicators over to the side, from the mattresses, from under hospice blankets, from the tents, the makeshift dormitory.

"Hija, this is the fullness of freedom," the man continued. "No hippie commune produced this. It's better than the most insolent rap. Any pornographic mosaic from Pompeii pales before this. It can't be compared to any Parisian watercolor of phalluses and vulvas from the nineteenth century. Your table dance is nothing next to this. These are real swingers. And look where it all takes place, in this very ass—and the city has many—just a few blocks from where liberals from Canada and Finland stroll, every one of them wanting to invent a happiness machine, and *whoa!* This is the kingdom of primitive Christianity, without any initiation rituals."

He pulled a tin from his brown habit and inhaled. Nausícaa saw him blush and it dawned on her that she'd never fully glimpsed the face of the other priest, Father Diego Tonatiuh, which was always hidden under the pointed hood.

"Are you coming over for dinner, hija? We live in the same building. I prepared something. Cous cous with a guajillo chili marinade and chili morita, spiced with epazote and yerba santa, fusion cuisine."

The altar boy with the small brazier appeared, scattering dirt and toluene around the fornicators. The neighborhood's residents curled up to sleep, hotels cautiously opened their doors. The local dives turned down their music to an intimate proletarian hum. Unaware of having lost a war—only one, and on Mexican land—San Fernando continued on his altar carved by Indians.

Nausícaa wanted to hang herself with San Francisco's pebbly cord until Father Próspero explained that the altar boy was the pastor of his congregation out in the streets, the one who chose the lambs whose souls would go to Chichihualco, Limbo, Tlalocan, Seville, or wherever.

Commander Pérez completed his part in the death of the queer cannibal. A hate crime, pure homophobia perpetrated by officially sanctioned killers. The guilty were predetermined. A patrol car took the commander home to a garish marble-and-aluminum subdivision with swimming pools and a golf club. His wife was sleeping. He gave her a kiss. He went to his children's bedroom, tucked them in. They'd left him their notebooks, as always, so he could check their homework. He went to his mahogany-walled study, with its diplomas from the Mossad and FBI, each framed by ninja stars. He reviewed the homework; he never let his kids down. He threw himself in an easy chair to watch *Law & Order*—he had the entire series on DVD—and tried in vain to read *The Odyssey*, his only book, which he owned in seven different editions. He had never read anything else in his life. Now an hourglass indicated it was time to deflower Nausícaa, of the snow-white arms, with his declaration of love: *Who takes you as a wife is the boldest of all. No mortal, neither man nor woman, has ever come before me like this, overwhelmed me like this at mere sight.* That very dawn he would tell her; that night they would leave for Cancún. He would buy a table dance and they would fuse orgasmically right there on stage. Oh Nausícaa! If only she'd already returned from the nave.

He left again for San Fernando, this time without escort.

"We are like angels; God made us, but not to marry or reproduce. Unlike the others, we were created individually—he put us in the hands of a surgeon so that each of our parts could be modeled, considered. We are neither cherubs nor seraphim; we don't marry or reproduce. We are simultaneously impersonal and celestial, but adventurous when it comes to sex. We are expelled from paradise and, because we live in Mexico City, we make rounds with the spirits of Huitzilopochtli, a brotherhood which San Fernando curses and about which he can't do a thing, even though his spirit comes to us from Seville. We are like the native witch doctors who have the ability to change into other beings, because God is fanatical, hija."

Father Diego Tonatiuh was hiding in a corner behind the altar, next to the photo of the dead bank robber disappeared by the state police. The decomposed corpse had been discovered unrecognizable in a sewer's foam. A red battery-powered lamp illuminated the photo, which was signed by *Sister Reckless of the Nuncas*, nicknamed *La Conversa*.

The priest walked through the nave to the choir, crossed himself under the cupola with the Immaculate Conception surrounded by angels with violins, lauds, and zithers. In the Expiatory Chapel, he said the Xochicuícatl: *"Begin, singer. Play your flowered drum. Delight princes, eagles, and ocelots. It's only for a brief time that we are on loan to each other."* He went to the inner door in the darkness shot through with lights, undid the bolt, and let the shutters fall on each other. He entered the confession booth and waited as he had on so many nights since he'd first seen Nausícaa in the neighborhood. *On loan to each other*, the phantom of the nuncas said to himself, immune to the blackness of the kettle in which his resentments were boiling over. *The time we're on loan to each other is so brief.* The bank robberies had only been emotional crises, prequels to a loving eternity that had disgusted Commander Pérez when he saw the effeminate lover in a cell in that wretched police station. Father Diego Tonatiuh sucked rancor from the depths of his hatred, let slip the rest in threads of saliva that thickened the broth of his miseries.

Nausícaa entered the furnished apartment building next to San Fernando. The façade had slumped from all the quakes. The waning moon lit the four-story stairway, nahui-four, a tangle of steps, a bridge of silver and obsidian between Seville and Tenochtitlán, Paradise and Mictlán.

"This is Mexico City, officer," said the altar boy with the brazier, who appeared on a landing. He was holding a bundle of dirty laundry smeared with the glue used by the congregation he shepherded. Father Próspero's door was open at the end of the hall. It was an anonymous wasteland like so many other apartment buildings. It smelled of lard, yerba santa, onion, chili peppers, and thyme. The girl entered her apartment dizzy from the smell and the altar boy's expression when he recognized her as the cop she'd once been. She cried sitting on the single bed; there was a thick Formica table, a hot plate, a piggy bank, a suitcase filled with clothes from the street market, her dancing lingerie.

She searched but didn't find her 9 mm. On the bilious and peeling wall, there was a photo nailed with thumbtacks of Commander Pérez embracing her, back when she was a he. They were dressed in black. Neither smiled. The bathroom door was open. The tiles were soiled, the shelf and her cosmetics, the mirror and the toilet. A single naked bulb cast shadows that darkened the skin. The commander had told him that his stay here would be temporary, only while the hormone treatment took effect so that nobody would notice the changes. But he never came back. He had food delivered from Chinese restaurants. She accepted the order not to leave until a messenger brought her an envelope with the address for the table dancing. She danced Monday to Friday, heading home in a cab at the end of each show. They paid her enough. She didn't need the extra money her colleagues made by taking clients to hotels. She was a virgin. She spent her weekends looking for company inside the bathroom. The more Nausícaa's eyes moistened, the more the space absorbed her emotions and became filled with the emptiness that she exuded . . . She didn't dare flush the toilet and empty it of the nothingness accumulating there in the bowl.

Bang! The shot rang in the nave of San Fernando as if it were from an ancient rifle instead of a Browning 9 mm. Three and a half centuries of walls cushioned the shot. The altar boy tolled for the dead in the bell tower. When Commander Pérez had come in search of Nausícaa, he'd found the door of the church slightly ajar. He'd been drawn to it. He'd pulled it open to let his corpulence through.

"God is fanatical, hija."

This was the nasally voice Pérez heard when he'd first entered the darkness. He had removed his pistol, aimed, and the echo had bounced off the columns of the altar, flown toward the vault, fluttered in the choir.

The cop still couldn't figure out where to point the barrel.

"God is fanatical, hija, that's what the Creator, whatever It is, will say to your beloved when It sends him to Hell." The voice was coming from a drain to the River Styx. Commander Pérez remembered it now. It was the same person who had claimed the bank robber's body. It was a woman who had transformed herself into man, wearing a nun's skirt, a black coat, and a priest's collar—he had seemed back then like a boy in his thirties, his adolescence bizarrely extended. The commander's obscene sense of smell had drawn him to the river, where some children led him to a dam, to the swollen body laying there in the foam. He hadn't officially registered the body, which had begun to decompose. The nun, or whatever it was, then threatened to tell the Vatican about the theft of the gold keepsake. But the cop had nullified the threat with an offer of papers that would accredit him as a priest anywhere. In the days that followed, the corpse crumbled apart in the dirty water like pastry dough. Sister Reckless didn't try to salvage the body, but her apparent indifference was in reality an expression of her abiding love.

"We have a deal, you demonic whore. I made you a priest. Nausícaa gave you the papers herself."

"I haven't forgotten. I chose the Castilian monastery at Cantalapiedra, which is a Claretian convent, though none of that mattered squat to them since you gave me a forged passport. So I returned to San Fernando a man, thank you. What I forgot was the deal itself. I agree, I broke it."

"What do you want, you filthy nun? Do you want to send me to jail because I killed your pathetic lover?"

"My resentment is blacker than the darkness of this church."

"Where is Nausícaa?"

"You're looking for her in the wrong place. She's around the corner. As always."

"The church door was half-opened."

"Or half-closed. Go on your way."

The cop turned, each swell of darkness illuminated by

candles forming a niche of shadows. A voice told him: "*There is no greater pain than to remember happy times in misery.* That's not me, commander, but Dante, and your misfortune is not having had any happy times, and your tragedy is realizing now, in this instant, that you will never have them, nothing to remember, and that in itself will become an eternity like a shot in the head."

In Father Próspero's kitchen, the altar boy finished shredding the meat from the street urchin. It was dawn. The priest sliced cheeks, guts, and eyes for a cocktail, escabeche style, to go with the cous cous. Hunger had given these delicate creatures big apple cheeks. The altar boy went outside to throw the viscera in a ditch. Exhausted from all her weeping, Nausícaa sniffled quietly in her own room and sought refuge in the bathroom. The priest hummed, chose a red onion, coriander, white vinegar, salt, enough lemon juice to clear the foul odors, cleaned the jalapeños, sprinkled black pepper with his thumb and index finger, waved some aromatic herbs, and got everything ready for the marinade. The altar boy returned with the news that there was a dead body inside the temple, surrounded by police, uniformed and plainclothes. "They won't have had breakfast yet," said the priest with the torn sneakers, so that the boy would prepare lunch for them. First, however, he needed to tell Nausícaa to go down to Father Diego Tonatiuh's confessional wearing a veil like María Magdalena.

Morning arrived downtown, and the children of the desert slept in the hope that the sun would wake their agonies in the open grave. The church door was wide open, but the passage to the shadows of San Fernando was blocked by yellow police tape. Nausícaa lifted it to step inside as two uniformed officers looked on indifferently at her purple table-dancing veil. She carried the guilt of the falsely devout. She crossed herself three times. Commander Pérez's corpse lay at the other end of the nave, the open sleeves of the raincoat making him look like a spoiled angel. A group of dusty judges stood to the side of the pulpit with Saint Michael and the stolen spear.

In a confessional down the other way, a red light flashed. *Stop!* the priest called out to Nausícaa, raising the sleeve of his habit, a light in the midst of a storm guiding the shipwreck as the tide moaned.

"The angels on the cupola are happy," said the shadow of the priest, gesturing toward the slipping light. Nausícaa collapsed when he removed his hood. He dragged her into the confession booth, where he sat and she knelt; he lifted her face to him. "Why are you here?"

"For my confession." Behind the opacity of her pupils, there was a view of a tiled and sticky room upstairs at the police station, the sound of Commander Pérez's laughter and boasts about how he'd handled the electric drill like a skilled swordsman. Nausícaa had admired the way he grabbed her head and forced her to lick the bank robber's nobler parts. The two cops outside the booth had a mutual orgasm, then basked in the silence of their brotherhood.

"No, Nausícaa, you have already confessed everything. The rape of the maid's son isn't even worth a Mass. You've come to return the borrowed spirit whose body is no longer among us. You sent it down to the sewers, to that Great Canal that cleaves this city like an infected vein, through which runs the waste that equalizes all of the inequities of those who live here. You couldn't take my lover, and you wanted me to lend him to you because, oh, how aroused you got when your big man fucked him up the ass! Cry now, you cheap whore—you're the only case I know of a rapist whore. Scream, you hag!"

Father Próspero came through the sacristy wearing dark clothes, his Roman collar, and tattered shoes. The altar boy set a table in the Expiatory Chapel, incense smoke trailing his small steps through the many pews of the nave. The police surrounded the priest. His waxen face shone. A commander said something about drug trafficking while the organ on high played, *Pange, lingua, gloriosi corporis mysterium, sanguinisque pretiosi*, and the rest of the conversation became inaudible. The officer who was speaking had taken part, along with Commander Pérez, in the investigation of a sacristan who, years before, had been assassinated while stealing an eighteenth-century gold talisman. The murder suspects were Próspero and Diego Tonatiuh; the police never returned the gold.

The altar boy served the vegetables. He set out chips with escabeche, cous cous tacos marinated in guajillo, and morita chili spiced with epazote and yerba santa. A detective brought cognac and Coca-Cola. The last bit of smoke from the incense slithered from the confessional.

"*Only for a brief time are we on loan to each other*, said the elders, back when this was a lake and the volcanoes had to always be watched. My penance will be the pain of remembering happy times during the misfortune, but you won't even have that." Father Diego Tonatiuh paused to catch his breath, then continued: "My loan was never complete, but during the bank robberies I had moments of happiness, even if I was only stealing for love. *Your* loan was never approved, and you were always unhappy. So go do your penance. You will never find the child you're looking for. You don't have your commander anymore, they're going to cut you to pieces during your table dance, and you won't have any way to make a living other than becoming a street walker. You certainly won't be able to afford your hormones. When your beard starts coming in again, no one's going to give a shit about you."

Mimicry flows like beauty from Mexico City's faucets, space and time are relative, and instead of the usual floral-and-stone façade, there's dahlia and obsidian. In the course of time, what was yesterday a lake of water becomes asphalt today, and the past is a perpetual duplication that drowns the future. Yesterday's omens come back, the same substance in a different shape. The city is a nagual that becomes a wall of skulls, an intelligent *domotique* structure: the Huitzilopochtli temple in a cathedral and Castile roses in cactus bouquets. Time is measured simultaneously with the Aztec, Julian, and Gregorian calendars and the cesium fountain atomic clock; the heart of Mexico City is made of mud and green rocks, and the God of Rain continues to cry over the whole country.

Father Próspero died from toluene inhalation. Father Diego Tonatiuh catechizes monks in the mountains of Songshan in China. The altar boy with the small brazier has grown a beard and moved east. More than five hundred years ago, Emperor Moctezuma was brought a heron with a mirror on the back of its head. In the reflection, the tlatoani saw bearded white men on red deer coming from where the sun rises. The altar boy returned mounted on a Harley, ordained a Franciscan in Cantalapiedra.

Through the west door's empty vestibule comes a ragged bearded woman with a turbid glance, shedding dirt like those thin pigs that don't eat anything but mud and grass. Her skin is a sallow olive. She sits on the floor, ignores the glue-addicted kids with vacant expressions, raises her eyes toward San Fernando, purses her lips with each breath, and shrugs off the tightness that causes such sorrow in her hormone-free chest. She smiles with a thin line of spit at the little winged angels that offer San Fernando to the winning king of the pagans in Úbeda, Jaén, Baeza, Cordova, Seville, defeated by the spirits of New Spain. None of the angels in the temple façade is the boy child she'd hoped to find. Behind the threshold, a different altar boy in a ragged habit sets down the small brazier; the incense drowns in the nave. The boy moves up to the tower, rings the bell, and tolls for the dead.

OF CATS AND MURDERERS

BY VÍCTOR LUIS GONZÁLEZ

Colonia del Valle

I t's hard to write about cats after Cortázar's Teodoro W. Adorno; Kipling and his cat who walks by himself; Poe's black cat; Hemingway's, who runs in circles in the corner; Lewis Carroll's cats. Therefore, since I've set out to write about cats in the next few hours of confinement, I will touch upon some facts involving my own cat: Wilson (that's the name I imagine represented by the W. before Adorno in Julio Cortázar's story) was yellow and big. Despite being fixed, he covered a lot of ground and would disappear for days at a time. When he returned, after he ate and drank plentifully, he'd sleep eighteen hours in one stretch. I imagined him telling me where he'd been and who he'd seen, including these four cases: Sinué, the Egyptian cat who lived with a neighboring family and had been run over at the corner of Patricio Sanz and Popocatépetl, torn in half when he tried to expand his territory. Did I remember the gray cat from the house across the street, the one with the gemstone necklace? He probably disappeared, precisely because of the necklace, after he sniffed a female and set off toward Félix Cuevas, where he then took a little jaunt down Amores Street. It was perhaps best that he not tell me what they say happened to the chunky little kitty from the corner, the one who used to like to cross Insurgentes Avenue and then Manacar theater and beyond. Good thing Wilson was fixed: no females and no territorial ambitions.

Then there was the fourth cat, the one belonging to a neighbor who was a foreigner—like me—an old and lonely American. During my stay in the snooty district called Colonia del Valle, this guy didn't talk to any of the other neighbors and actually had some sort of problem with most of them. It was during the early '80s and he had been there almost twenty years. He had a Mexican wife, who left him after more than a decade and a half of ill treatment, and they had two tall blond children who, because of their looks, acted untouchable and could have become telenovela actors. I began to know too much about this neighbor just before my return to the United States. Events in Mexico had conspired to destroy me in three short years, and they were about to complete the job when I filed for bankruptcy and my responsibility with my family's businesses ended.

After Papa's death and during my mother's supposed terminal illness, I was forced to leave my academic life in Dallas and return to Mexico City. Alice wanted to go with me because she wanted to find out about my family's businesses. According to our divorce agreement—which wasn't yet final—she would get half of whatever I inherited. To be frank, we should never have gotten married. It happened because, as it turned out, Alice always believed that if she were going to marry, it should be to her best friend. Over the course of time, only our friendship survived.

As soon as we got to Mexico City and Colonia del Valle, she got the house in order, prepped rooms for both of us, discovered that most of the neighbors wanted to get to know her (as usually happens with foreigners in this country), and began to work on her Spanish. She bought Wilson from the veterinarian at the San Francisco street market. The kitten struck me as too big to be a newborn, and I am pretty sure I saw him smile after his first bottle of milk at our house. In a year, he had become the evolutionary link between the saber-toothed tiger and the domestic cat.

From the start, Alice got in the way of my having women friends, in spite of her easygoing demeanor. I told her, "I don't understand what you're doing here, in Mexico, with me, in this house; if you were a drunk or a drug addict it would make more sense." Her answer was always the same: it had to do with our friendship and her interest in finding out how much she was entitled to of "man's earthly goods," or, in this case, woman's. She said she'd finish dealing with my parents' businesses and properties in Mexico and then we could each go to our own *sancho*. "Santo, Alice, the word is *santo*." She said she'd heard that you could say *sancho* too. Well, yes, but that was something else entirely.

In fact, the only person on our street, and on *any* streets for that matter, with whom our foreign neighbor maintained friendly relations, was Alice, whether it was because she was also a gringa, or whatever. It was like she was the only person the neighborhood mad dog wouldn't bite, something doubly strange given the antagonism between them: for example, one day, annoyed by the loud music coming from the neighbor's house, she called him and, after identifying herself and asking him to stop his "scandalous behaviour," she insulted him in English for several minutes. This rant—at times completely incomprehensible to me, thanks to my being from a higher social class than Alice—began with the phrase "With all due respect" and finished off with the old American favorite, "Have a nice day." As soon as she hung up, she said, "Stupid old man," but she wasn't angry anymore; she was on the verge of laughter. Quickly, she added, "Better watch out, he told me he was going to break my husband's face."

One morning, I spied Alice through the large living room windows talking with somebody out in the park. The sun was strong and, because of her height and the light reflecting off her blond hair, it took me a moment to identify the gringo. They were chatting without the slightest trace of hostility.

"What were you talking about with the neighbor?" I asked as soon as she returned to the house.

"He's a vulnerable old man," she replied.

In those first days in Mexico, the process of liquidating my family's businesses was frequently bogged down by my ignorance. I didn't have a sense of the bigger picture, and this caused tremendous paranoia: as far as I was concerned, the partners, lawyers, and accountants were a gang of conspirators trying to rip me off. Besides, my mother—whom I stopped believing was on her death bed when I saw her playing golf after just one week in the hospital—had signed over power of attorney to me so I could do whatever I wanted, which I considered confirmation of my suspicions that, rather than dying, she was merely retiring, and was unloading everything on me. I canceled the sale of stocks, reinvested dividends, raised wages, and upped benefits as an act of revenge, just as neoliberalism arrived in Mexico with the new president, Miguel de la Madrid; I washed my hands of any possibility of profit and figured things would crash when they needed to crash. Alice just shook her head. I had given her an update on the family businesses at a less-than-ideal moment.

The night before, believing she was still away on a trip, I came home with one of the company secretaries directly after a little office party. That next morning, Alice showed up in the breakfast nook, dressed to play tennis. I was forced to introduce her, so I gave her name, and she added, "His wife." The secretary almost spit out her coffee; immediately, she blurted, "What a big cat, and what huge fangs!" Wilson stopped rubbing himself against Alice's thighs and moved toward his dish. The secretary asked "my wife" if that was her natural hair color. They started chatting as if they had studied fashion and makeup at the same school. As she left, the secretary said again, "What an enormous cat!" I told Alice about the party and the change of plans with the family businesses. She shook her head. I explained that the partnership would benefit from the privatization policy with which Miguel de la Madrid was ridding the nation of its excessive goods, handing them over to the domestic and foreign bourgeoisie; that the profit from the divorce would be even larger. None of it went over well with her.

"If you're going to continue bringing your *viejas* . . ."

They aren't actually very "old," I explained to her.

Did I always like café-colored women?

"Alice, we say *morenas*—brown, if you like."

"Well, if you're going to keep sleeping with them, at least be sure I'm not at home."

Later, just as I was sliding my car out of the garage, a young man started attacking the gringo. I jumped out of the car and shoved the guy before he began to kick the old man. The gringo got up and, after spitting and wiping some blood off his face with the sleeve of his shirt, growled at me to stay out of it, that it was none of my business, and then he called me an idiot. *What?*

A couple days later, I found Alice and the gringo having coffee and chatting amiably in our living room. I greeted her with a kiss and she said, in Spanish, "You remember him, he lives next door?" ("We say *neighbor*," I whispered.) I remembered him, of course. I made eye contact with the old man for a passing second. Then I locked myself in the study. Alice soon appeared with a drink for me, took a seat on the rug next to the armchair where I was reading, and hugged my legs.

"You know," she began, "I think that cabrón killed somebody, perhaps many people, and I don't mean in a war. He's like a serial killer."

"He's gotten away with the murder. In Spanish we say, *he got away with it*, Alice." Of course, there was no need to ask why she thought this: it was female intuition. "They almost killed him the other day," I said, and I told her what had happened.

"Ah, yes," she responded, apparently aware of the incident, "that's how it is with his kids." Alfonso, the handyman on our street, had told her about worse incidents, even shootings; he'd never been hurt badly, but imagine the shock. "Did you know that Wilson fascinates him? He likes cats. He has a kitten now, he doesn't know what kind, but she's spotted. He actually named her Spots." *How imaginative*, I thought. "He says she has a face like a whore, a made-up whore," Alice laughed, "like in *Cats*. And she wears a flea collar. But when the gringo tried to pet Wilson, he clawed the guy."

"We say *scratched*, Alice."

Things changed, or went to hell, after that day. When I think of it now, it's as if I woke up and the new situation was already there, just waiting for me to open my eyes.

I grew anxious as I headed out to the garden. There was a short ladder up against the garden wall, which I would have to climb in order to leave food and water for Spots.

A few days before, I'd woken up in the middle of the night and met her. I'd seen some branches move through the bedroom window—a rustling of leaves on the garden wall—and thought it was Wilson coming back from a night of mischief. But what emerged from the weeds instead was a spotted kitten, with a flea collar and the face of a whore; she took a few steps around the cornice when—suddenly—Wilson appeared behind her. Frightened by the sheer size of the "saber-toothed tiger," Spots fell on her back. Wilson simply watched and smiled.

That same morning, Alfonso, the handyman, had knocked on my door and asked, on the gringo's behalf, if I'd seen a spotted kitten in heat. It was impossible to know for sure (of course, that same dawn, I'd suspected, by virtue of the meows and shrieks outside my window), but the possibility of more than one spotted kitten wandering the neighborhood was remote: she had to be his cat. What was the plan? Alfonso shrugged his shoulders. Just imagine, I said, how difficult it will be to catch a female in that state. "If she were human, at least I'd have a chance."

How many weeks had it been since Spots deserted her house and began subsisting on the water and croquettes I was leaving for her on top of the garden wall? Time had lost its coordinates since Alice made her final trip back to Texas, and marks on calendars and clocks meant nothing. I suppose I could calculate the months since I'd come home with company and Alice was still there, her flight canceled. This time it wasn't a coffee-colored woman but a European, as blond and tall as Alice. They had looked each other over as I introduced them, and I'd considered it a good sign that Alice didn't feel the need to clarify our relationship. I'd already decided to sleep with the European. "Will you excuse us?" I was on my way up the stairs when I heard about the canceled flight; she'd try to book another in the morning.

Alice went away and didn't come back. On the phone, in Spanish and with Mexican irony, she recommended I do whatever I wanted; it was my life, after all, and she was no longer interested in my well being or whatever earthly goods she might be entitled to in the divorce.

I put the ladder up against the garden wall and took another drink for courage. I began to climb, holding a bowl of croquettes; I was stretching to place it on top of the wall when I was knocked back by a sudden weight collapsing on my neck; I scratched at the air, my back slammed down against the turf. It was better not to move for a bit. I breathed. Wilson climbed on my chest, cuddled up, and quickly fell asleep in spite of the drizzle. How many more kilos had he gained in the past week?

A court decision forced me to deal with business matters and discover that my partners had cheated me out of my share. Lazy in the comfort of her pension, my mother, in a tone of retroactive warning, said, "The idea was to sell over time, hijo." According to her, I had my father's tendency to think I was clever, like most gringos in Latin America. Then she issued another warning, this time in a more severe tone: "And don't sell the house!" Although it was already mine and I had power of attorney, it would be best to claim it as an inheritance when she died.

The truth is, I'd already sold it. Twenty days before turning in the keys, I went looking for a carrier to take Wilson back to Dallas with me. (The only suitable one I could find was actually designed for rottweilers.) I boxed things up, dealt with the furniture, and packed my luggage.

One wretched Saturday afternoon, it grew cold outside and looked like it was going to rain. I wanted another drink but couldn't find a single drop in any of my bottles. To top things off, not even the cat was home. Then I heard him when he dropped onto the roof of the shed, and by the time I got to the garden he was already coming down the trunk of the palm tree, his second stop before touching ground. I grabbed him by an eyetooth and carried him up to my room, where I let him loose and closed the door. "Stop trying to crawl under the bed, you already know you don't fit," I advised. So he jumped on the blankets, curled up, and pretended he was asleep. Very well. I looked for his brush and began to comb his head. I remembered that the sonic frequency of a cat's purr is capable of destroying cancer cells.

A few nights later, much worse—after another bad calculation regarding the content of my bottles—the screams coming from Spots no longer sounded like she was in heat. She was hungry and cold. After my fall, I was no longer enthused about climbing to leave her food. She'd been on her own for the last week. When I could, I'd leave croquettes for her on the roof of the shed, but it wasn't easy for her to get up there. Wilson invariably finished her rations.

That night, however, I heard Spots jump from the garden wall to the roof of the shed. It was a dull thud, weak in comparison to the thunder from Wilson's heavier impact. Wilson began dozing while I went out to investigate. I ascended the ladder, and there was Spots, eating what was left of the croquettes. She saw me and immediately began flirting. She meowed and purred and rubbed her body on the roof. I went back down for a slice of ham, returned, and tossed her a small piece. She ate it quickly, so I tossed her another. Each time, I dropped the pieces of ham a little closer to me. I talked to her about the weather, I told her it was cold and that it would rain again soon, and that it'd be better to go home or allow herself to be caught. The stepladder started shaking and I could hardly maintain control as Spots munched away. I suddenly lunged and caught her by the flea collar and was able to grab the scruff of her neck; I don't know how I managed to avoid falling with that cat. There were kicks, scratches, howls; looks that said, *I will never trust a human being ever again.* I wanted to snatch the phone and the neighborhood directory at the same time, without letting go of her. I ended up using Wilson's rottweiler carrier. That's how I should have begun.

There was a gun collection on the wall. A huge rifle with a scope. No hunting trophies. The gringo seemed proud of his little mahogany bar lined with bottles. He fixed cocktails for both of us. Instead of toasting, he merely said, "Boozing time."

Drinking hour, I said to myself, and then, like him, I nearly downed the full cocktail in one swig.

He asked about Alice. Her? Fine. I would be going back to the United States soon. I pointed to the carrier in which I'd brought back his cat. That's for transporting my Wilson. The gringo finished another drink. I did the same.

"I've never seen a bigger cat," he said. I agreed: if he were any bigger, he'd be in some museum as the live part of a Paleolithic diorama.

Not a muscle moved on the man's face. His gaze was intimidating. There were moments when I wanted to leave, but another drink—or perhaps my fear of simply excusing myself, grabbing Wilson's carrier, and taking off—kept me in my seat. I had a feeling that the old man was using my visit as an excuse to start some kind of party. From the moment I arrived with Spots, I noticed an eagerness that I first thought was relief at his pet's rescue. His offer of a drink seemed natural under the circumstances, and fortunate, given the alcohol deficiency at home.

The gringo left his place by the little bar and moved over to his turntable. He put on a record by an American band. "You like Miller?" he asked without smiling, and then took a couple of dance steps, also without smiling.

"Yes, of course I do."

He turned up the volume and pressed some buttons, concentrating on equalizing the sound. I looked with greater focus at the wall with the gun collection. One could almost imagine the sudden appearance of a red deer or buffalo head. In their place, I noticed photographs; the light from the little bar barely reached them.

I frequently think back to what happened during those three years in Mexico, and especially that night. Imprisonment in a Texas jail provokes obsessions that wouldn't develop in other places, I suppose, including other jails. Here, the looming presence of death row and its dead men walking make for a different atmosphere. The proximity of the execution room and the condemned bring the past to life, the one that ends here.

Up close, I could see that the photos were of the gringo when he was young: as a soldier in the Second World War; dressed in civilian clothes, next to armed companions; receiving a trophy and, below, a sign that said *The Perfect Marksman*; finally, standing next to a freshly shot animal. There were also photos of John F. Kennedy: with Marilyn Monroe, with Sinatra, with his brother Robert, when he was in the military. Even one in which Kennedy looks like a cadaver, he's so thin. And one more, a picture of Kennedy next to his wife in a convertible; below it, in an arduous scribble and barely legible in the weak light: *Dallas, Texas*, and the date, *November 1963*. The gringo appeared behind me and asked if it would bother me if he repeated "American Patrol." No, I replied, then returned to my seat. I was talking carelessly, fueled by alcohol and my host's silence; the fact that he wasn't saying anything made me anxious. He was one of those people who hide their emptiness in silence. I spoke about Kennedy, alluding to the photos on the wall; I noted that not even the government's commission investigating his death had been able to prove in any credible way that there was only a lone gunman. I talked about Alice, how we'd stayed friends even after we married; about Wilson and his ability to smile. I had my hypothesis: this would be the next ability that cats developed in human society; smiling, let's say, as an extension of purring. An evolutionary leap to become even more desired and nurtured by humans. A resource, a new survival strategy. The gringo looked on, shrugging his shoulders. When I talked to him about Kennedy, I thought he'd at least explain the photos, but he barely blinked. He seemed to get more interested when I first mentioned Alice, but faded again once it became evident I wasn't offering any intimate details. I only remember him saying one complete sentence: "So you're Texan, from Dallas, right?" I thought it would lead to something, but he simply kept drinking.

I went back to Dallas, our divorce was finalized, and Alice and I went back to being just friends. Once more, back to classes and routine, until Wilson disappeared for a couple of days and then somebody left his wet corpse on the porch. I was told he'd been drowned by one of the neighbors: taking that delicate delight, so American, in abusing the weak, the neighbor had allegedly submerged Wilson in his pool and amused himself by not letting him back to the surface. I wondered if Wilson had tried to smile at him along the way.

One morning, I crossed my yard over to my Texas neighbor's pool; I found him swimming with his family. I shot him before he could come out of the water.

Alice's jail visits usually mean news. A "horrific" earthquake had destroyed Mexico City. The first neoliberal president, Miguel de la Madrid, had initiated a period—who knew how long it would last—of more Mexican misfortunes. My mother continued to play golf. One of the gringo's sons beat him to death, but the TV station for which he worked paid for a defense that set him free. There was no news about Spots. Wilson's killer recovered from the shooting, was well for a while, and then had a cardiac arrest; he suffocated from a lack of oxygen in his blood. I was glad, I was very glad.

RENO

BY JULIA RODRÍGUEZ
Buenos Aires

I agreed to meet up on a damn Saturday with my childhood pal El Floren—that's what we called him cuz he was
from Florence, a town in Tejeringo el Chico . . . no, not
really, I'm just messing around—and my compadre Chente,
who I hadn't seen since I baptized his kid—actually, that's not
true either—and my cousin Teobaldo, a.k.a. The Clone, his
brother-in-law, a guy known as El Pirañas, and another guy
I didn't know, older than the rest of us, very big and thick-
lipped and scary, nicknamed San Beni, San to his buds. Our
usual territory—that is, the places we lived for short periods
of time—was Buenos Aires, Obrera, Tránsito, and part of that
Apache zone in the city center.

You get so sick of having to scramble to make a buck that
you just put on your best face and take what you can get:
sweeper, bricklayer's apprentice, spontaneous electrician,
dressing up like a bullfighter to sell pins to tourists, bank security guard—well, not that, because then you have to fill
out that stupid application where you have to list all your
names and tell them if you have a criminal record, if you've
had chicken pox, how long you've been unemployed and why,
provide a letter of recommendation and explain what you've
been doing for the last five years—so no, no, and anyway, why
stand in line for that pathetic little job that no one wants to
give you anyway?

Because living in Mexico City, the Capirucha, the Defe—whatever you want to call it—living here, but not in the nice neighborhoods like del Valle, Florida, San José Insurgentes, San Ángel, Polanco, the Hills, and, nowadays, Santa Fe, means being taken advantage of by everyone, including the big-cheese owner of the main telephone company, because that's been poor people's turf forever, and now it's becoming the Beverly Hills of the Defe, which just fucks with my head; it's like having a picnic in the middle of an interstate, or intentionally walking against the traffic up Calzada de Tlalpan.

We agreed to meet that ill-fated Saturday at the Poblana, a brewery and family restaurant in Doctores. Happy to see each other again and already quite drunk, we took an oath like the Musketeers and decided to stop being poor, to do whatever it took to live free.

It's hard living in the shitty neighborhoods, with the exception of Tepito, which just needs this much to become a neighborhood of loafers absorbed into a larger city filled with more of the same. Being marginalized means being jobless: sometimes it means no water, sometimes it means no food; often it means having to hang off a lamppost just to watch a little TV, or knowing the bodies you have to step on to find a place to sleep. It's being able to fall down drunk on the street, as the case may be, or taking a shit right there if your body demands it. It's freezing cold and too much heat, floods, rockslides, depending on the season and the place; it's the perpetual absence of authority, unless, of course, someone wants to fuck with us. It is, I'm telling you, total crap.

As time went by, two of us began taking our chances with the passengers on the Allende metro at the Chabacano, Portales, and Pino Suárez stations. As we got to know the territory, we got in the groove with the local sharks, and everything was love and happiness. My buddy Chente doesn't like crowds because he starts to sweat, his throat gets tight and his vision hazy, so he doesn't participate in this type of merchandise exchange, but that's no prob, we all share with each other and we take care of him. He, like El Pirañas, prefers to do business at the ATMs in the nice neighborhoods. There's good "food" there, says El Pirañas: there aren't many people, they're very civilized, and there's no need to get stressed out—the clients always cooperate, meaning they put up with El Pirañas' bites. My cousin Teobaldo is an ace when it comes to identity theft and he's raked in good profits from that. El Floren is into auto parts and pretty much anything anybody will buy. I serve as a special assistant to everyone, depending on the work, but always with San Beni, who's the bodyguard for the others during their operations.

At one point I had sunk so low that I was willing to do *anything* to bring home the bacon. Even the biggest nobody has his responsibilities, whether it's the mamacita, the brother, the old woman (and someone else you might get cozy with on the side) . . . then there's the arguments over money with the in-laws, the brothers-in-law . . . piles of problems, and fuck, there's the matter with the shorties some woman brought to the crib. This is the basic minimum level of crap, though sometimes it's a little better: the diapers, the baby bottles, the vaccinations, the schools (if the kids even get in). And the books, notebooks, pencils. And bus fare, rags to wear, quinces celebrations, weddings, funerals . . . and I'm exhausted. That's why I think what happened happened.

As it was, our small business was moving along on greased rails and we began to see things differently. I found myself laughing over pretty much anything, San Beni began playing with his grandson, who at this particular moment he just wanted to throw off the balcony. Floren hooked up with the sexiest woman in his neighborhood; this actually provoked so much envy in Buenos Aires that he had to borrow a friend's Volkswagen to avoid people seeing him when he went to visit her. San was finally able to buy a gym membership to stay in shape, and Chente's wife took him back. What more could we ask for?

But, you know, there's always a fly in the ointment or a bug in the rice, and Beni got pissed at some roughneck from his neighborhood who started spreading the rumor that he was a faggot—thus the focus on his biceps and triceps. I never imagined that Beni, so thick-lipped and big, could be that vindictive. With us, he'd always been a child of God: he never raised his voice, never uttered an obscenity. He'd say, "Boys, why do you have to talk like truck drivers and spit like those trashy street hustlers?" He was very decent, very courteous, he even washed his hands when he went to the bathroom. He couldn't drink, that's for sure, but he was good with his hands; he was like a fine embroiderer the way he could put together or take apart anything he had in his fat fingers. But whenever he got drunk, he started talking about his childhood, back when he was a good boy. You can't imagine the kinds of horrible things that haunted him as a former daddy's boy. The thing is, he decided to get rid of the rumormonger via the guy's woman, with the objective of also putting a total stop to the gossip.

One wretched night he summoned us as witnesses to an abandoned auto shop in one of those neighborhoods I was talking about before. It was almost dawn. He'd managed to get the girl to come with him—she was tiny but had a pretty face; he'd found her in a bar. "I have a life-or-death message for your man," he'd told her, and really, after that, who wouldn't go with? Then, in that auto shop, everything got so intense and we each took turns. But later . . .

I don't really want to remember what happened later; everyone did whatever. In the end, San Beni turned out to be more of a bastard than a pretty boy and we had no choice but to get rid of the mess. And there we were, stressed out but half asleep, trying to figure out how to end the story.

If it hadn't been for my cousin The Clone—that moron made a deal with his gossipy sister-in-law, the one who sells tamales outside the Coyoacán station—I wouldn't be here, in the RENO prison treatment center (which is nothing like the low-security CERESO), all freaked out about falling asleep next to my friends and their stench. It's a smell, I swear on my mother, that never fails to provoke a recurrent nightmare in which my buddies are forcing me to eat painted fingertips inside Chiapas-style tamales.

ABOUT THE CONTRIBUTORS

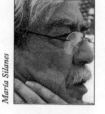

EUGENIO AGUIRRE (born in Mexico City, 1944) won a Great Silver Medal from the International Academy of Lutèce, France, for his historical novel *Gonzalo Guerrero*, and a José Fuentes Mares literary award for *Pasos de sangre*. He has published more than forty-five books, including volumes of short stories and Mexican best sellers such as *La cruz Maya*, *Isabel Moctezuma*, and *Hidalgo*.

ÓSCAR DE LA BORBOLLA (born in Mexico City, 1952) is a very popular writer of more than a dozen short story collections. He has a doctorate in philosophy and teaches university metaphysics.

ROLO DIEZ (born in Junín, 1940) is a two-time winner of the Hammett Prize, and winner of both the National Prize in Literature and the Gran Angular Award for young adult novels. His published works include *Los compañeros*, *Vladimir Illich contra los uniformados*, *Gambito de dama*, and *La carabina de Zapata*.

BERNARDO FERNÁNDEZ (born in Mexico City, 1972) won the Memorial Silverio Cañada prize in Spain for best first detective novel for *Tiempo de alacranes*. He is also a comic book artist and the author of several sci-fi works, including *Gel azul*, which won the Spanish Ignotus award for best science fiction novella in 2007.

VÍCTOR LUIS GONZÁLEZ (born in Mexico City, 1953), novelist and journalist, won the 1988 Juan Rulfo International Prize for best first novel with *El mejor lugar del infierno*.

F.G. HAGHENBECK (born in Mexico City, 1965), won the 2006 Vuelta de Tuerca prize for the best first detective novel with *Trago amargo*. He also writes for popular American comics, such as *Crimson*.

MYRIAM LAURINI (born in Santa Fe, 1947), one of the very first female noir writers in Mexico, is the author of *Morena en rojo, Que raro que me llame Guadalupe*, and *Para subir al cielo*.

JUAN HERNÁNDEZ LUNA (born in Mexico City, 1962), a two-time winner of the Hammett Prize for best Spanish-language detective novel, has published more than a dozen crime-fiction novels, including *Quizá otros labios, Cadáver de Ciudad,* and *Tabaco para el puma*.

EDUARDO MONTEVERDE (born in Mexico City, 1948) won the Rodolfo Walsh Prize for the best nonfiction Spanish-language book for *Lo peor del horror*. He is also the author of two experimental noir novels, *Las neblinas de Almagro* and *El naufragio del Cancerbero*.

ACHY OBEJAS is the translator (into Spanish) for Junot Díaz's Pulitzer Prize–winning novel *The Brief Wondrous Life of Oscar Wao*. She is also the author of several books, including the highly acclaimed novels *Ruins* and *Days of Awe;* and editor of *Havana Noir*. Obejas is currently the Sor Juana Writer in Residence at DePaul University in Chicago. She was born in Havana.

EDUARDO ANTONIO PARRA (born in León, 1965) won the 2000 Juan Rulfo International Prize. *Los límites de la noche* and *Tierra de nadie* are among his many published works.

JULIA RODRÍGUEZ (born in Mexico City, 1946) wrote one of the very first Mexican noir detective novels, *¿Quién desapareció al comandante Hall?*

Renata Vega-Albela

PACO IGNACIO TAIBO II (born in Gijón, Spain, 1949) is the founder of the Mexican neodetective story, author of more than fifteen crime-fiction novels published in twenty-eight countries, and three-time winner of the Hammett Prize. He is the author of *Cuatro manos (Four Hands), Retornamos como sombras (Returning as Shadows),* and *La bicicleta de Leonardo (Leonardo's Bicycle),* among others, as well as the Héctor Belascoarán Shayne mystery series.

Marina Taibo